Praise for

Kicked Out

"Boasting down-to-earth, believable characters and pacy action, Dassu's intensely readable sequel to *Boy, Everywhere* . . . deals squarely with the racism and intimidating bureaucracy facing young refugees." —*The Guardian*, **a Book of the Month**

"This is a story of friendship, resilience and hope, and while Dassu doesn't shy away from the horrors of racism and the refugee experience, she spreads a message that everyone, including children, can do something to help. Uplifting and powerful." —*The Bookseller*, **Editor's Choice (also *The Bookseller* Buyer's Guide: Ten [Books] Not to Miss)**

"Warm and perfectly observed. Dassu writes the best child characters out there—flawed, messy, cheeky and utterly believable."
—Louie Stowell, author of *Loki*

"A powerful and empowering portrayal of hope against adversity. A. M. Dassu is one of our most authentic voices in children's literature."
—Hannah Gold, author of *The Last Bear*

"A heart-warming, empathy-inspiring tale—and a call to action—deserving of a place on every good bookshelf." **—Dr. Graham Fairweather, senior school librarian**

"*Kicked Out* will inspire young people to become involved in social activism and capitalize on the positive difference that they can make in their communities. Another great book with powerful and important messages at a time when we really need them." **—Kevin Cobane, high school teacher**

"An absolute must read!" **—Sajeda Amir, high school teacher**

Praise for

Boy, Everywhere

★ "Disrupts stereotypes while tugging at readers' heartstrings. . . .
Compelling, informative, hopeful." —*Kirkus Reviews*, **starred review**

★ "This isn't an easy read, but it's an absolutely essential one."
—*Booklist*, **starred review**

★ "Strongly evoked themes of family, homesickness, and friendship cohere in
this resonant portrait of one teen's contemporary refugee experience."
—*Publishers Weekly*, **starred review**

"Essential reading for middle grade students and anyone hoping
to gain insight into the plight of refugees." —**Book Riot**

"A gripping, uncompromising debut, super-charged
with the power of empathy." —*The Guardian*

"A fantastically well-researched and empathetic story that gives humanity
and respect to those seeking sanctuary, busting a number of stereotypes
about refugees along the way." —**Amnesty International**

Kicked Out

Books by A. M. Dassu

Boy, Everywhere

Fight Back

Kicked Out

A. M. DASSU

Tu Books

An imprint of LEE & LOW BOOKS INC.
New York

Copyright © 2024 by A. M. Dassu
Jacket illustration copyright © 2024 by Daby Zainab Faidhi

TU BOOKS, *an imprint of* LEE & LOW BOOKS INC.
95 Madison Avenue, New York, NY 10016
leeandlow.com

Manufactured in the United States of America

SUSTAINABLE FORESTRY INITIATIVE

Certified Sourcing
www.sfiprogram.org
SFI-01681

The text paper is SFI certified.

Edited by Stacy Whitman
Book design by Sheila Smallwood
Typesetting by ElfElm Publishing
Book production by The Kids at Our House
The text is set in EB Garamond
10 9 8 7 6 5 4 3 2 1
First Edition

Cataloging-in-Publication Data is on file with the Library of Congress
ISBN 978-1-64379-687-1 (hardcover)
ISBN 978-1-64379-688-8 (e-book)

For everyone who felt they weren't worthy or good enough because of the way they were treated by others.

You are enough. You just need to see it for yourself.

Kicked Out

Chapter 1

I typed over a selfie of me in front of my best mate Mark's massive pool and shared it on my Snapchat story. I grinned, looking through my camera roll at all the goofy photos of Sami and Mark splashing each other. I didn't think I was *ever* going to get used to how supreme Mark's new place was. Life had totally changed since his mum won the lottery.

I picked up a slice of toast while still scrolling through my photos at the kitchen table. You'd never have thought from looking at them that Sami wanted to run off back to Syria just a few months ago because he hated it here so much. It was so good to see him having fun. We'd clicked like we'd always known each other. Spending time with Sami and Mark always made my day, and hanging out in a massive mansion with a heated pool on a school night made every minute *even* better.

I was selecting a video of all of us shoving lots of cookies in our mouths to post on Snapchat, when someone snatched the slice of toast from my hand.

"Oi!" I turned.

"I'm running late for uni! Make another one!" Samira, my big sis, waved her hand at me dismissively as she walked out the kitchen.

"*You* make yourself one!" I shouted.

"I've got a revision session for my next exam and you're just sitting around, so no." She slipped into her shoes in the hallway, opened the front door, and left.

"Here, have mine," said my little brother, Ahmed, scraping his chair back from the kitchen table and pushing his plate towards me. His brown hair was as messy as ever and he was still in his *Minecraft* pajamas.

"Why you not eating?" I said, taking his leftover slice.

"I had some Doritos." Ahmed shrugged.

I made a face. Stinky crisps first thing in the morning was a whole new level of yuck.

"Are you going to Mark's again today?" Ahmed said, glancing over my shoulder at my phone.

"Yeah, man!" I said, midbite.

"Can I come?"

"Errr, no!" I swallowed and swiped out of my camera roll. "You ain't ever hanging 'round with us. You better get that idea out your puny eleven-year-old head now!"

"Not fair!" He huffed and walked out of the kitchen.

I went into WhatsApp to message Sami to find out how long he'd be.

"What's not fair?" Mum walked in with a basket full of dirty laundry.

"Life, innit, according to him."

Mum lifted her kameez from the hem so it wouldn't touch the floor, before bending down and loading the washing machine. "Oh, Ali, make sure you pick up Ahmed from football practice tomorrow. The optician can't reschedule my appointment, so I won't make it in time."

I gobbled up the last of the toast. "I can't," I said with my mouth full. "Samira will have to do it."

"She's revising for her exams . . . and you, my dear,

have nothing to do." She shoved the last of the clothes in and clicked the door shut.

"Yeah, I do! I'll be at Mark's, and it's well far. By the time I get there, I'd have to come back!" I pushed my chair and got up.

Mum poured washing powder into the compartment. "Ali, you were at Mark's house after school all of last week! You're going to be there all day today. You can spend Sunday at home."

"Not the whole week. This will only be my fourth time!"

"Only!" She turned and smirked. "Only FOUR times in ONE WEEK."

"Well, it's amazing." I put my phone in my back pocket. "*You'd* be there every day too if you saw it." I still couldn't believe that Mark's mum had actually won the lottery and moved them from a tiny council flat, where the whole housing estate looked the same, into the most mind-blowing place.

"Take me to see it, then."

She pressed the start button on the washing machine and picked up the empty gray laundry basket, then tucked it between her arm and her bright pink kameez.

"I can't do that!"

She turned around and grinned. I wasn't sure if she was serious or not.

"You need to tell Mark's mum to have a house-warming party for the Year Eight school mums!"

"Oh my God, no way!" I headed to the door.

"Wait, Ali."

I turned.

"Make sure you pick Ahmed up tomorrow."

"But—!"

"Shhh, no buts. With your dad not being around, Ahmed needs you to be there for him. You know I wouldn't ask unless I had to. I *have* to get my eyes checked."

I sighed. Because of my loser dad, I had to be the "man" around the house. Even though I was just barely thirteen. I wondered what life would've been like if Dad hadn't left us all behind as if we were stale milk. Maybe he'd be having breakfast in the kitchen with us. Maybe he'd have dropped me and Ahmed at footy practice like the other dads did.

Stop. Block the thought, I told myself. *He's not worth it.*

"So, you'll get Ahmed, yes?" Mum asked.

"Yeah, yeah, OKAY!" I had to step up 'cause *he'd* stepped out. Mum had me. "I'll get Ahmed."

"Thank you, my gorgeous laddu!" She came over and pinched my cheek.

I leaped back and looked at her in horror. "What the—? I'm not two anymore!"

"You're the man *and* one of the babies of the house."

"How does that even make sense?"

She chuckled. "Well, you're the man of the house, but will always be the baby of my heart."

I forced a frown so she'd stop and headed to the door. Mum was hilarious.

"Here, have some barfi."

I stopped in my tracks and turned.

Mum pushed a box of milky sweets on the table towards me. "Rubina's son got engaged, so she sent these to mark the occasion."

"Which ones are they?" I popped the red cardboard lid open.

"The plain ones you like. Not a pistachio in sight."

"Ohhh, yeaah!" I pinched a block of creamy barfi out of the box.

"Ey! Don't take a whole chunk! You're supposed to cut that!" Mum tutted.

"Well, the baby of your heart has to eat!" I said. I popped the whole thing into my mouth and the taste of cardamom danced on my tongue as I chewed on the soft, crumbly rectangle.

Mum shook her head, smirking, and I hurried out of the kitchen and ran up the stairs before she thought of *another* chore for me.

The doorbell rang just as I got to the top. I sighed and ran back down and opened the front door.

It was Sami. "All right?" I smiled, still chewing down the barfi. "You're early. I thought you were running late?"

He unclipped his bike helmet. "Yeah, I thought I would be 'cause Aadam went off on one after getting a letter from his lawyer about—"

"Where's big bro?" I looked around Sami, into the street.

Aadam wasn't really Sami's big brother; they'd met somewhere on their journey from Syria, and now he lived with Sami's family and was like the brother Sami never had. To be honest, he was like a big brother to all of us. Aadam was sixteen, but just so much more grown up and with it. I'd rather have had him as my older sibling than Samira, but I'd never dare tell her that.

"He's gonna go straight to Mark's house from the lawyer's." Sami bit his lip and shifted.

"Oh cool, we'll see him there then."

"Nah, we probably won't." Sami shook his head. "He's gonna be busy. Mark's mum messaged to say she'll pay him a full day's work 'cause she wants him to do the whole lawn today. She's gonna do a barbecue or something." Sami pushed his floppy hair off his face and hung his helmet on his bike handle. "You ready?"

"Yeahh, man! I'll just get my swimming stuff."

≡

We got off our bikes as we turned on to Mark's road. Actually, Mark's *private* road. That's what it said on the street sign. We'd always get off and walk up the long, pretty, tree-lined street, so we could gawp down the deep driveways and catch a glimpse of all the mansions.

"Hey, is that Aadam?" I said. A tall dark-blond teenager in joggers and a gray T-shirt was strolling along up ahead. His black rucksack had a Syria flag stuck on the front compartment.

Sami cupped his hands around his mouth. "Aadam!"

"'Course it's him. Ain't no teenagers 'round here,"

I said, looking at Sami. We'd seen no one else our age on the street all week. It was probably full of old, rich people.

Aadam turned, smiled, and walked back to us.

"How did you beat us here?" asked Sami.

"I got a lift!" He pulled on the strap of his rucksack.

"From who?"

"This guy from Syria who was at the lawyer's too."

Aadam spotted me and put out his fist.

I bumped it. "What's happenin', bro?"

"Ah, got problems, akhi."

"Nothin' some football after school won't fix." I smiled. "I know you're working all day today, but join us again tomorrow?" Even though Aadam didn't go to our school—in fact, he didn't go to school at all right now and instead worked under-the-table jobs, when he should've been doing his GCSE exams—whenever he had the time, he'd meet me, Sami, Mark, and the other guys from our school footy team in the park to basically thrash us. Although he'd call it "helping you train."

"No, this time it is serious problem," he said, in his Syrian accent.

"What's up?" I asked.

Sami looked down. Okay, so this was not good.

Aadam sighed. "I got a letter from Home Office."

"Home Office?" I stared, waiting for him to explain.

"Yeah. The immigration department—they reject my asylum application again."

Oh man, I'd just talked all over Sami earlier when he'd tried to tell me about Aadam's lawyer. I thought he didn't look right but got distracted when he'd mentioned Mark's garden.

"But you did an appeal and everything!"

"Yeah, and the judges decided I wasn't . . . how do you say it?" Aadam looked at Sami. "What was the word in the letter?"

"Credible." Sami shifted his feet.

"Yeah." Aadam faced me. "They say I'm not believable because I got my dates wrong about when I left Syria. I said one date in the statement when the man at the homeless hostel helped me fill in form and then a date before in the interview with Home Office . . . Just one day difference! I was stressed; I didn't remember dates! And now they say I'm not credible." He dropped his shoulders and sighed, his mouth drooping into the saddest curve.

Sami looked up. "The letter also said you said the wrong name of the street the mosque is on."

"Yeah." Aadam blinked hard, as if he was annoyed with himself. "I was panicking in the interview, so I forgot. It was like a big test, and they made me talk about what happened to me on my journey and I was upset and not thinking right." His voice shook and he bit his lip.

"Worst thing is even the judges said they believe the Home Office that he's an adult." Sami shook his head.

I gasped. "How can they say you're an adult?!"

Aadam showed me his leathered hands. "They say my hands are too wrinkly for sixteen-year-old. I tell them I have eczema and it's because I was homeless on the streets for months and my hands got worse, but they don't believe me." Aadam shrugged and shoved his hands into his pockets as he walked alongside us.

"So, hang on." I glanced at Aadam. "They're saying you can't stay here anymore?"

Aadam nodded. "I have fourteen days to appeal the decision, but my lawyer said it's not going to pass because of weak evidence in my application and we will have to do a fresh claim. But other problem is I have run out of free legal aid because he spent so much time on my case already. So now I have to pay lots of money to my lawyer to do this and to prove I am sixteen . . . I need three to four thousand pounds, and I only have one hundred!"

"What happens if you can't pay him?"

"Government will deport me."

I stopped dragging my bike, and Sami and Aadam stopped too. "What, send you back to Syria?"

"Yep," said Sami. I now noticed the dark circles under his eyes. They'd probably been up late talking about it.

"But it's not safe!" I said, a bit too loud.

"The government don't care!" said Sami. "They just want him gone."

Aadam sighed loudly and walked off. "I better go. Don't want to be late for work."

"Oh man, wish you could join us," I said after him.

Aadam shrugged. "I need to save all the cash I can. Got to keep head down and work every chance I get!" He started jogging away.

"We'll see you there," Sami said.

"Hey, Aadam!" I shouted, and he turned. "Don't worry, man. We'll figure something out, yeah?"

Aadam put his thumb up as he continued to jog down the road. He worked so hard, even though he was only sixteen. It wasn't fair.

Sami glanced at me, and I nodded at him. We had to do something. There was no way we could let Aadam get deported. He'd only just made it here in one piece. God knows what would happen to him if he went back.

Chapter 2

Sami smiled, even though his face looked sad.

"Are you worried about Aadam?" I asked, as a bird on a branch above me flapped its wings and flew off.

"Yeah." He sighed. "I don't know what'll happen to him if he goes back to Syria. The government will probably make him fight in the war. He could die . . ."

"Listen, yeah. That ain't happening. He is going to get that refugee 'leave-to-remain' thing like your family did. He ain't going nowhere."

Sami blinked long and hard. I could tell he didn't believe it. I suppose it was all too fresh for him. Life had only just got to some kind of normal after his own traumatic journey to Manchester earlier this year.

Sami's little sister had stopped speaking after she was in a mall that got bombed, and it was because she'd gone with his mum to get Sami some football boots. I think he still thought it was his fault they'd had to leave Syria. And on top of that, now he was worrying about having to lose Aadam after they'd only just met again in England a few months ago.

I looked through the black iron gates of the house we were passing and tried to distract him. "Was your house like this in Syria?"

"No!" Sami laughed. "We weren't that rich! We lived in an apartment building. Most people in Damascus do, but ours was a nice stone one and we had a small garden too." He glanced at the houses. "There *are* huge houses like this, but they're further up the mountain and belong to all the government people and superrich."

"Oh right . . . So no pool then?"

"Nah! I wish! We used to go to an outdoor one that was open to everyone. I've not seen one like Mark's." He grinned.

"I don't think anyone we know has!" I said.

Mark's pool was next level. It was a huge rectangle shape that ended in a semicircle. It was lined with bright blue tiles that made the crystal-clear water reflect onto an arched, painted ceiling above, making it look like the sky. It had six floor-to-ceiling stone pillars on either side of it, and the wall that was attached to the kitchen side had arched mirrors, so the pool looked twice its size. The wall on the semicircle side of the pool was all glass doors that looked out onto the garden, and all the floor tiles were heated.

Sami's face had brightened. I'd cheered him up. Phew.

A few weeks before Mark had moved, we were ecstatic because we'd all made it onto the school football team. We'd been in the park every day after school, practicing drills to prove we were worthy of being on the team, but we lost the chance to go through to the next round of the County Championships. Then Sami had been made captain because Nathan, the previous captain and also a total thug, got dragged for being a racist and was demoted.

Nathan was Sami's archnemesis. Actually, mine and Mark's and our teammate Elijah's too. Pretty much half the school football team's. He was like the Joker, and all of us were more like Batman—obviously. He'd wanted us all to worship him as our team captain, but he was a bully and basically a racist crudhead.

The promotion to captain for Sami could not have happened to a better human. With Nathan demoted, things were finally looking up for us, and to top it off, Mark had moved to the best area in the whole of Greater Manchester: Hale Barns, where people had spotted Manchester United footballers . . .

We pulled our bikes up to Mark's front gate. I looked at Sami and grinned, thinking back to our first day here and how amazed we'd been to see Mark's new house. We knew in that very moment our evenings and weekends were about to change.

"Wait, is this number twenty-seven?" I'd asked Sami on that first day as we stopped outside the biggest house I'd seen in my entire life.

"It must be," Sami had said, his eyes all googly, wide and sparkling. He'd pressed the silver entry buzzer on the wall next to the humongous iron gates. "Mark's mum has got some good taste, man!"

"Come throooough!" someone who sounded like Mark had said through the fuzzy intercom, and then the gates started slowly opening inwards. We waited for them to open wide enough to let us through and wheeled our bikes onto the long, neatly blocked, paved driveway that led to a sweeping staircase going up to a perfect house with four big windows on either side of huge wooden double doors.

"All right?!" Mark had said as he held the front door open and beamed.

Sami and I had just stared. The front lawn was perfectly trimmed, the trees were perfectly sweeping in the breeze, and the birds were chirping pretty perfectly too. It was all just so . . . perfect.

"Are you kidding me?" I'd said, fist-bumping Mark as we entered a marble hallway facing a staircase that split into two upstairs. A bit like a Disney palace.

"I kid you not. Mum actually did this!" Mark laughed and splayed his hands on either side of him.

"Check out your shooooes!" Sami pointed at Mark's Air Jordans. "Are those the latest ones?"

"Yeah!" Mark kicked up one of his black Jordans and showed off its red sole.

"They're awesome," said Sami. "Like this house. Is she gonna buy it?" Sami looked up at the high ceiling and crystal chandelier hanging over our heads with his mouth wide.

"I think so. She said we'll be renting it for a few months first, until it all goes through."

"Are those cameras?" I'd pointed at a white ball in one of the ceiling corners.

"Yeah, that's CCTV. It's everywhere except the bedrooms and bathrooms."

"I didn't think I'd *ever* see anything like *this* in real life," I'd said, peeking into one of the large rooms on the left with polished wood floors and a huge marble fireplace.

I heard some footsteps and glanced back into the hallway. A man who looked like he spent every waking hour in the gym *and* under a tanning bed had come down the stairs, wearing a fitted black vest and tight white shorts. "These the mates you wanted over so bad?" he'd asked Mark, looking straight through us.

Mark had jumped as soon as he'd heard his voice. "Yeah."

The man grunted as he passed us, his shoulders hunched like a Neanderthal's, his hands fisted. It had looked like he was trying to show us how ripped his muscles were.

As soon as he'd gone into one of the rooms, Mark had whispered, "That's Callum, my mum's new boyfriend. He's a bit . . ."

"Rude?" I'd said.

"Scary?" said Sami.

"Yep, both those," confirmed Mark. He'd waved us to follow him. "Let's go to the pool. That's gonna be *our* place."

≡

I remembered how my stomach had twirled as we'd followed him through a massive kitchen with enough space for a corner sofa AND a dining table, and then into the big indoor pool room. A heated pool we could swim in all year round. It had felt like the perfect end to the school footy season. We only had to wait a couple of months until the summer holidays started, and then we'd be spending the whole day here, not just after school and on weekends. We were gonna live the high life, like proper footballers did. And it was gonna be epic . . .

I pressed the silver buzzer on Mark's gate for the fourth time, my insides bubbling just like they had that first day. This was going to be the best summer ever.

Chapter 3

I dive-bombed into the pool, holding my breath and letting my body plunge to the bottom before bursting out of the water, gasping. I looked around for Sami and Mark.

Sami shoved loads of water in my face, and I turned away before going full force and splashing the heebie-jeebies out of him. Mark joined in till none of us could see anything but water spray, like the back of a speedboat. When the crashing of water went quiet all of a sudden, I stopped and peeked. Mark was swimming to the edge of the pool. His mum was walking towards him, smiling, in sparkly heels and a floaty pink dress. I'd never seen her so dressed up. Before they moved here, she was always in joggers and mostly frowning. Man, a big lottery win really *could* change everything.

I swam to the edge of the pool, where Sami was now sipping Coke from a paper cup he'd left on the side.

"Mum's ordered margherita and chicken feast pizzas, that okay?" asked Mark as his mum closed the double glass doors behind her.

"Oh, thanks! We can't eat the chicken one though," said Sami.

"She's ordered them from Roosters; I told her to," he said, sitting at the edge of the pool and slipping back into the deep end. "They're halal—right, Ali?"

"Yeaaah they are. Thanks, man!" I said, doing a somersault in waist-high water. Not a good decision. I surfaced with my ears blocked and my throat feeling scratchy. Why'd I never remember it always felt manky coming back up?

Sami climbed out of the pool, dripping his way across the tiles and up two steps to the table Mark's mum had set up for us, which looked out at the garden. He eyed the ten or so fizzy-drink bottles and picked up a fresh paper cup. I swam over and climbed out onto the warm tiles that felt as if I was standing on the baked sunny earth in my nani's front yard in Pakistan. How was it even possible to heat tiles like this?

Aadam was outside on the ride-on lawn mower. We'd begged him to let us have a go on it every day he'd been here. Mark had suggested Aadam could tidy the garden while his mum found a proper gardener, since they didn't know anyone in this new area, and it worked perfectly for Aadam in between his evening English classes and other odd jobs he did for cash.

"Imagine if he'd just let us drive it," I said, joining Sami at the table.

Sami finished pouring Coke carefully into his paper cup, making sure the fizz didn't go over the top, then handed me the bottle.

"Oh, yeah, I forgot to tell you—we've got to stop asking him that," he said before turning to see where Mark was. Then he leaned in to me. "Aadam got really irritated with me last night and said he can't risk losing this job. Well, you know why, but also, Mark's mum's boyfriend has been keeping an eye on him and is freaking him out a bit."

"Seriously?" I poured myself a cup.

"Yeah."

"All right," I said. "It's not like we could properly

drive around anyway, 'cause we'd probably ruin the grass."

We watched Aadam doing the lawn in silence. I put the Coke bottle down and glanced at Sami. "I thought your dad was gonna do the application for Aadam to live with you guys and it was all gonna be okay?"

"He couldn't." Sami sighed. "Because Aadam had already applied for asylum when he was at some homeless hostel before he met us, and you can only have one application at a time. My dad helped him to appeal the Home Office decision, but they've said no again. They're saying his case is closed."

"What does that mean?" I chugged down my Coke, the bubbles popping all over the back of my throat as I swallowed.

"He's basically got one more chance to say they've made a mistake, but if they say no again, then he's gonna get deported. But his lawyer said they're probably going to reject him, and he will have to apply from scratch again because of the mess he made in his interview, plus his first application was not strong because he had no paperwork. He needs to get more evidence this time." Sami pointed to Aadam with his Coke cup. "The main problem is he has to pay this time because he's making the same application again in one year, and so he won't get any free legal help."

"And they charge so much."

"Yeah," said Sami.

It all sounded so complicated. Something no kid should ever have to think about. I couldn't get my head around the government saying Aadam was an adult just because his hands were wrinkly and he seemed a bit mature compared to most sixteen-year-olds. He had to be mature to survive everything he'd gone through the last couple of years.

I heard a big splash behind me and turned. "You want some?" I said to Mark, holding up the now-half-empty Coke bottle.

"Yeah, go on then!" Mark shouted, before swimming across the pool. Within seconds he was over to our side, even though the pool was massive and felt bigger than the swimming pool our school forced us to have lessons in every winter.

"Thanks!" said Mark, reaching out to grab his cup from me. I wiped my hand on the back of my wet shorts to get rid of the pool water he'd just dripped over it.

"Everyone must be superrich on this street, right?" said Sami, glancing over at Mark.

"No idea." Mark shrugged and took a sip of Coke. "I've seen one old person driving a classic car, but no one since. Anyway, the driveways are so long, I can't even see most of their front doors."

"Yeah, but have you even left this mansion and walked around since you moved here?" I asked. "Is all your stuff from the old place here now?"

"Nah," said Mark. "Mum said she didn't want to take anything from the council flat. She said she wants to forget we ever lived there, so she gave everything to charity. Too many bad memories."

"Actually," said Sami, "he *has* left the mansion."

"When?" I said, taking a glug of drink. Aadam had now finished this side of the lawn and was driving off to the bigger one further behind.

"When he went to get his BRAND-NEW RANGE ROVER!" Sami shouted. His eyes always sparkled when he talked about cars.

We all laughed.

"Oh, yeah, I forgot!" Mark said. "It's here! Come, let's go see it!"

We put our cups down on the table together and turned to see Mark's mum come through the door that led to the house with a stack of pizzas on her arm.

"Hello, boys, they just delivered them." Her voice

echoed as she strutted down the four marble steps. We ran over to meet her halfway, our bare feet pattering on the warm tiles.

"Here y'are," she said, smiling.

"Thank you!" I said, taking a box, and Sami said the same as he took his. Mark took the final box and his mum put a tub of coleslaw on top of it.

"God, it's hot in here." Mark's mum knelt down and touched the floor tiles. "Did you put the under-floor heating on, Mark?"

"No," said Mark. Mark's mum had told him off about the heating being on in May the other day. It looked like she was going to tell him off again, but this time, they were interrupted.

"Gemma!"

We all looked behind Mark's mum. It was her new boyfriend, Callum. He ran down the steps in his baggy jeans, T-shirt, and—wait, were they Gucci shoes? Yeah, beige shoes with "GG" all over them.

He frowned as he approached us all. As he got closer, I noticed his T-shirt said:

I AM NOT A RACIST . . .
I Just Don't Like You!

Was he wearing that because of us?

"You got them *three* pizzas! What you doin'?" He glared at me and Sami from head to toe in disgust.

Ugh. Look at him, I thought. *So glad Mum didn't get married again after Dad left. Imagine dealing with this kind of grief every day. Poor Mark.*

Callum didn't even try to hide how much he hated me and Sami. Otherwise, why would he wear that T-shirt and look at us the way he did?

"Oh it's all right, there's plenty more," said Mark's mum. "After having a bare fridge for so long, let my boy eat properly with his mates." Mark's mum smiled at us.

"I need to show you something,' he said, tugging her elbow. He put his arm through hers and led her away from the pool.

We all rushed back to the table and set our pizzas down.

"One . . . two . . . three," Mark said, and we lifted the lids off our pizzas together. The hot cheesy smell made my insides groan as if I hadn't eaten for ages—even though I'd had toast just over an hour ago.

"How come you moved your dad's picture out of the hallway?" I pointed at the framed photo of Mark's dad leaning against the tiled wall behind the table.

"I didn't. Callum did." Mark looked down.

"And he put it on the floor?" Sami's mouth dropped. "Won't it get damaged by the moisture in here?"

"Probably wants it to. Callum said it gave him the creeps and it might attract ghosts." Mark shrugged and took a bite of pizza.

I stopped myself from rolling my eyes at the stupidity of that explanation.

Mark had been the first person to make time for me when I'd joined Heath Academy halfway through Year Seven. His dad had died in a car accident a few years before, when Mark was still in primary school. We'd clicked and become good friends after he'd asked our teacher, "What if you don't have a dad, Miss?" when she'd asked us to write about our families. Mark was just the nicest guy. He missed his dad loads, but like me he'd got used to it and just got on with it because he knew he had to be there for his mum. He didn't deserve *this*.

"He told Mum he'd put it up on a wall in here 'cause I'm in here so much, but still hasn't."

"Is he being weird about other stuff as well?" asked Sami, picking up a slice of pizza from his box.

"Yeah . . . You see his Gucci shoes?"

I nodded, taking a bite of pizza.

"He made Mum buy him them for his birthday, which is not for another month. They were seven hundred pounds!"

"No way!" Sami gasped.

"There's definitely something up with him," I said. "D'you think he's here 'cause . . . your mum won . . ."

"All that lottery money? Yeah, kinda . . . But I've not seen Mum this happy for years, not since Dad . . . so I'm not saying anything. I don't want to ruin it for her. She'll just think I'm being jealous or something." Mark waved his pizza slice around as he spoke. "Plus, I don't really have any proof he only wants her money. He's nice to her most of the time. She's always laughing with him." Mark shuffled his feet. "And he was with her *before* she won the lottery—even if it was just for one week. He didn't know she was rich then." Mark looked at us as if he wanted us to agree. "Just a shame we've got a big house now and he thinks he can just move in all of a sudden. Can't even say there's not enough room like I did when he wanted to stay the first few nights in the council flat."

It was obvious Mark was finding this whole situation hard. I punched his arm gently.

"Shall we go play some footy after we've ate?" said

Mark, changing the subject and looking out at Aadam, who was now tidying up next to the bench outside.

"Shame Aadam can't join us," I said taking another bite. "Do you think he could after he's finished doing the garden?"

BANG, BANG, BANG.

I looked up midbite. Mark was knocking on the glass doors and waving Aadam over. Aadam dropped his rubbish bag and glanced up. Mark waved harder, and Sami and me joined him at the doors. I waved my pizza slice.

Aadam strode over, smiling and straightening his T-shirt over his joggers. His blue eyes gleamed in the sun.

"You want some?" Mark asked, pulling the doors open and pointing at the pizza.

"Yeah, thanks! I'm so hungry." Aadam took a slice from Mark.

We all turned to a crashing sound behind us. Mark's mum and her boyfriend burst through the doors.

"GET OUT!" shouted Callum, pointing at the patio doors behind us.

Sami's eyes widened and Mark's jaw dropped. I stopped chewing.

Mark's stepdad/mum's boyfriend/whatever he was

marched down the steps, his chest out and legs wide. Mark's mum's face looked menacing, not the smiley one we'd seen just moments ago. I swallowed the remaining pizza in my mouth whole. Why were they angry with us?

Were they telling Aadam to get out? But he wasn't really inside. I suppose eating pizza on the job was probably a crime. Or at least a sackable offense. We'd have to own up and tell them it was our fault Aadam had stopped working. He couldn't lose this job!

"How dare you come inside *our* house and THIEVE?" shouted Mark's mum, with a black rucksack swinging from her hand. "I trusted you! I thought you were different!" She pulled wads of cash out of the bag and started chucking it onto the floor. "You wanted this, did ya? Thought you'd get away with it?!" Some notes landed on the tiles and some in the pool.

Huh? I looked around. What was she talking about? Why did she think we'd stolen money?

Hang on. Did she mean Aadam?

I turned and saw Aadam drop his pizza slice.

"AND WE GAVE YOU A JOB! GET THE HELL OUTTA HERE! NOW!" shouted Callum, marching over, his fists swinging.

Aadam ran. And I backed away.

I was just about to open my mouth, when Callum barked, "I told you, Gemma, they're all the same! These two probably helped him. They're lucky we found this money, otherwise they'd all be leaving in a police car."

I glanced at Mark, who was wide-eyed, his mouth still hanging open as if he'd frozen in time.

Callum clapped his hands on my and Sami's shoulders and forced us to turn to the open patio door that led to the garden. His fingers were digging into me.

"Now get out, and if you're lucky, you'll get your clothes back round the front," he said, shoving us hard out the door and then slamming it shut.

Chapter 4

We stood in the storm porch at the front of the house, mouths open. We had just been kicked out of Mark's house. His mansion. FOR STEALING MONEY WE'D NEVER SEEN BEFORE!

I couldn't believe it. Hot air burst out of my nostrils as I tried to calm my breathing.

Sami wrapped his hands around his bare chest and shivered. "So do we just go home now?" The previously sunny May sky had clouded over, and everything looked gray.

"What? No way!" I said, touching my hair to check how wet it was. It was dripping, and I was topless, only wearing soggy swim shorts. "We didn't even steal anything. That Callum hates us—it was obvious he always has from the moment we first came here. He's a nasty crudhead. Did you see his T-shirt just now? And he said 'they're all the same' and we 'probably helped him.' We ain't goin' nowhere."

I walked off barefoot down the nine stone steps and onto the cold brick driveway, looking up at Sami, still standing on the porch, dwarfed by the size of the house.

It was like we were outside the mansion from *The Fresh Prince of Bel-Air* in those reruns Mum made us watch, but the Fresh Prince in this case was my best friend, Mark. And we were in Hale Barns, not LA, and instead of Jazz, the not-good-enough best friend, me and Sami were the ones who had been kicked out.

RIP our pool day.

I considered walking back around the wraparound lawn to find Mark and get him to tell us what was going on.

"Who'd have thought today would've turned out like this?" shouted Sami from the top of the steps.

Not us, I thought. *That's for sure.*

I saw someone above the porch waving frantically from a window that was as big as the double doors below. Mark. About time!

Mark stopped waving as soon as he saw me running back up the steps. He turned around and spoke to someone. Maybe his mum?

His mum—she'd been so nice! Why did she let her boyfriend kick us out before explaining? I'd tell her we didn't steal any money and she'd sort it.

The front doors opened, but before I could even say hello, Mark's mum chucked a black rubbish bag out, followed by a pair of trainers. Sami ducked.

Just as he stood tall again, she chucked another pair of trainers and slammed the door shut. My Jordans!

I sucked my teeth and ripped open the knotted black bag to find our clothes.

"Gonna have to wear these unshowered," said Sami, smelling his shoulder as he held his T-shirt in front of him.

"I know, I feel nasty," I said, pulling on my white T-shirt and then my jeans on top of my cruddy wet swim shorts.

We both sat on the top step to get our socks and trainers on. It felt icky to put dirty feet into socks, but we had no choice. Sami hung his shoulders.

"Listen, we ain't leaving till we get our bags and an apology, yeah?" I said. "They'll find out it wasn't us and they'll have to say sorry, you watch. We don't know nothing about any money."

"Yeah, we just went straight into the pool room. What are they talking about?" said Sami, scratching his half-dry head.

The front door opened behind us, and my rucksack landed on the porch's stone slabs, followed by Sami's. Callum stood at the door and sneered.

"Don't make me come and force you to that gate!" he shouted. "LEAVE! NOW!"

Sami scrambled to his feet. I tried to look like I had a bit more courage and walked over to grab our rucksacks, even though I was actually worried Callum was going to come out and punch me.

The door slammed shut. I breathed out. After handing Sami his bag, I pulled out my phone and saw Mark had messaged. Thank God.

> M: They're saying Aadam took loads of money. About £5000. Callum found it in his rucksack in the boot room. Mum is fuming. Just go home for now and I'll call as soon as it's calmed down here.

"Aadam!" Sami shouted as he leaned in, reading the message. "Where is he?" He bunged his hoodie back into his bag and slung his rucksack over his shoulder, then stormed down the steps onto the driveway.

I ran to catch up. "Whoa, that's just madness ... five thousand pounds. He wouldn't."

"Aadam!" Sami shouted towards the back garden. I turned to see Callum standing on the porch, legs apart and his hands on his hips.

"Let's go," I said. "We'll call Aadam from outside."

We grabbed our bikes from against the wall, and Sami pressed the buzzer. Someone opened the gate for us so we could leave.

As soon as we got to the end of the drive, we spotted Aadam sitting on the curb near the corner of the street, his head down and arms hanging over his knees.

Sami didn't wait. "You didn't take it, did you, Aadam? Did you tell Callum about your legal fees?"

"Huh?" Aadam got up, looking confused. "That man scares me. I thought he was gonna beat me like the men in Lebanon, so I got out of there ... and they had my bag and were throwing money from it. I—I need to find another job, akhi," he said, his eyes wide and panicked.

"Aadam. They think you stole it from them!" Sami got in his face. Boy, he was angry. "Mark's mum's saying

Callum found that money in your backpack. Just tell me why it was in there!"

Aadam took a step back. His eyes welled and he looked wounded. He glanced at Sami for a moment and then at me, then turned and ran.

I grabbed Sami's arm. "Why'd you say that to him, man?"

"Because he's about to be deported!" he said, watching Aadam disappear around the corner out of sight. "You heard him, he needs about four thousand pounds. And they're saying he stole five. They've got the perfect excuse to blame him. What if he told Callum he needed money?"

"Sami, you didn't even ask him, man. You just went right in, as if you believed Mark's mum and her boyfriend over Aadam, your actual bro . . ."

Sami swallowed. "Oh man. Ali . . . I was just so scared for him and trying to get his side . . . What have I done?"

Chapter 5

Sami pulled out his phone from his jeans and dialed Aadam's number for the fifth time. "He's not answering, man! I don't wanna leave another voice message!" He rubbed his hand over his face in frustration and leaned into the bus seat.

"We'll try your house first, yeah?' I said over the loud whoosh of a truck that passed our window. I gripped my handlebar to stop my bike from tipping over. We'd decided we'd be quicker jumping on the bus, but bringing a bike on made the journey much more stressful, especially with all the evils some of the passengers were giving us. Man, it was hard to ignore those nasty looks.

Sami gripped the seat handle in front of him as the bus screeched to a stop, then started typing with both thumbs:

> **S:** I'm sorry akhi. I just wanted to get your side of the story.

Aadam pinged right back.

"Finally!" said Sami, before opening the message:

> **A:** I did not take anything. There is no story.

When the bus finally got to Stockport Bus Station, we had to wait for another bus to get to Sami's house. Sami tapped his foot, checking his WhatsApp every few seconds, waiting for Aadam to answer Sami's text asking where he was.

"How would he even have known where the cash was kept?" I said.

"I know, it makes no sense." Sami shrugged.

"Maybe Callum made it up?"

"Yeah, maybe," said Sami, watching an old lady walking past us pulling a trolley bag.

Once we'd caught the next bus to Sami's new neighborhood, we raced to his house. It was always awkward coming here because of the way everyone looked at us. As if we were going to rob them. Or already had. But it was better than when Sami had first arrived in the UK and was living with his cousin Hassan and his evil mum, even though that house was only a couple of roads away from mine. Things got better for him once he moved out of there. It was like he believed he could make friends and have a life in England, and he just chilled out more.

Sami ran into his house shouting for Aadam, while I waited outside with my hands in my pockets, hoping no one would jump me or take our bikes. I thought I'd better let Sami and Aadam sort things out first.

Someone tapped the window behind me, and I jolted. It was Sami's little five-year-old sister, Sara. She had her nose squished against the window, her chestnut-brown hair pulled back into two pigtails, and she looked even cuter than the last time I'd seen her. I waved at her, and she gave me a small wave back. I was just about to pull a face to make her laugh, when Sami dashed out. He'd been gone less than a minute.

"Aadam's not here," he panted, out of breath.

"So where next?"

"The library? He might've gone there to do his evening class homework?" said Sami.

We jumped onto our bikes and headed down the street to the main road, towards my neighborhood and the library. It was warm, and thankfully my shorts felt less soggy against my thighs as I rode.

We leaned our bikes against the wall in the library entrance area and raced through the barriers, splitting up once inside the main hall. I took the shelves section; Sami went towards the desk area.

"He's not here," I said, meeting Sami in front of the reception desk in the middle.

"Okay, the park," said Sami, heading back through the security barrier towards the doors.

Even though we hadn't taken any books, it always felt weird going through the barriers. I turned and waved at the librarian, like I had to show I hadn't taken anything without checking it out first.

We tried the small park near the library first and spotted Grace, our school Director of Sport's daughter, kicking a football around with her mates. We hadn't seen her, or any of the footy-practice lot, since Mark had moved to his mansion and we'd got distracted by the pool. It looked like she was still practicing in the park without us though. Even on a Saturday. If anyone was going to make it professional, Grace was. She was way more determined than any of us.

She grinned when she noticed us and waved us over.

"We can't!" I shouted.

"In a rush . . . We're looking for Aadam!" called Sami. "Have you seen him?"

"No, I haven't . . . All right, later!" Grace took the ball from her mate and dribbled it away, her long blond ponytail swinging side to side as she ran off.

We wheeled our bikes down the uneven ramp towards the gate.

Sami nudged me as we headed out of the park. "Are we still gonna practice with her and the others after school?"

"Yeah! It's not like we're gonna be going to Mark's to swim anymore. We got all googly-eyed with that pool. Shouldn't have stopped playing, man!" I swatted a fly off my arm.

"I'm not sure I wanna play for the school team in Year Nine next year."

"Seriously? You're the captain!"

"Yeah, I dunno if I want the stress of having to play with Nathan."

"Nathan can buzz off," I said, opening the park gate and dragging my bike out. "I reckon he'll never go for you again after the telling off he got from Mrs. Hack."

Me, Sami, Mark, and Elijah had shown our Director of Sport what Nathan was really like a couple of weeks ago. Still, he'd got into Sami's head by telling him he'd only made the team because he was a refugee and our coach had felt sorry for him.

Ever since then, Sami had questioned his own skills and whether he'd play on the team long term, even though Sami was now our team captain and we all got the joy of watching Nathan squirm at being told what to do at training.

Sami glanced at me. "The weekend's just flying by, man."

"I know . . . It's been well rubbish. Getting booted out of Mark's house like a pair of criminals topped it off." I sighed.

"Mark still hasn't messaged," said Sami, his voice almost drowned out by a passing bus.

"I bet Callum is still shouting at him." I squinted in the May afternoon sun. The clouds had cleared again, and it had warmed up, but I still felt as miserable as I had earlier.

"Where next to find Aadam?" Sami looked at me.

"Big park?"

"Yeah!"

We both rode towards the bigger park about half a mile down the road. I took a gulp of breath as we

approached the tree-lined entrance and walked through
the gates with our bikes. We walked under the cover of
trees, our trainers crunching the bark lining the path,
each step bringing up a musty, earthy smell. A squirrel
rustled through the bushes followed by a little white
fluffy dog with brown patches. I stopped, putting my
hand out to get Sami to stop too. I did not want to get
between a dog and his squirrel. We watched the squirrel
scramble up a tree trunk, giving us a side eye as it went,
the dog yapping after it.

The dog's owner came panting out from the side
path. "Buffy! Get here now!" She smiled at us as if to
say "Sorry, this is a thing." She grabbed the dog's blue
collar and clipped its lead onto it and led him away. The
squirrel was long gone.

Sami nodded at me, and we carried on walking,
grateful to be out of the sun and in the shade.

We went through the kids' playground, past the
snaking slide, towards the rickety wooden bridge.

Sami did a double take. "He's there!" he whispered,
and nudged me.

I turned and saw a dark-blond teenager with his
hands in his pockets, moping on the swings. A lady
with a big baby bump was pushing a squealing toddler
a couple of swings away from him.

When Aadam heard our footsteps on the wood chips, he looked up, wiping away a tear. My stomach dipped. This was not going to be good, man.

Sami dropped his bike and sat on the swing next to him, his head bowed. I wondered if I should just leave them to it but decided to sit on the last swing beside Aadam. I smiled at the happy toddler next to me in the baby swing.

"I didn't steal," said Aadam.

"Aadam, I'm sorry. Everything came out wrong. I know you wouldn't . . . It's 'cause the boyfriend said he found money in your bag," said Sami with his head still lowered.

"That's a lie! I wasn't even inside house!" Aadam shouted, and stood up. "I'm not allowed in the main house because I'm a 'worker,' remember? I haven't even seen a ten-pound note there. Forget five thousand pounds!"

He walked off, and we both jumped off the swings to follow.

Aadam turned. "And look at this." He pulled his phone out of his pocket and showed us a message from Callum:

C: U R FIRED. AND U AIN'T GETTIN PAID.

"So why didn't Callum say anything to me about it?" Aadam continued. "And why didn't they call police and get me arrested if they've got proof I stole so much money from them?" He shoved his hands in his pockets and marched off again.

Sami looked at me, and we both grabbed our bikes and rushed to Aadam, putting ourselves on either side of him.

"You're right, it doesn't add up," I said.

"Yeah, it doesn't," said Sami. "They kicked us out too."

Aadam slowed down. "Look, you know I need the money for legal fees, and five thousand pounds would pay for it *all*, but even then, I wouldn't steal it. I'm just sad you thought I would, Sami." Aadam glared at Sami and sped up again.

Sami bit his lip and stared at me.

"Why'd you say it, man?" I said, watching Aadam, who was almost at the edge of the kids' playground area. "You know him better than anyone."

"I said I was sorry! I didn't think he did! I just wanted to be sure..." He looked down. "One time, I almost stole some money from my dad to help Aadam get on a better boat from Turkey... so it's not like I wouldn't get it. When you're desperate, everything makes sense."

Sami slouched, dropping his head to his chest. His face was flushed.

Man, these two had some complicated history. "We have to go after him. Come on!" I said, jumping onto my bike.

"Aadam!" Sami shouted.

Aadam looked back and stopped just as he reached the open park gates.

"Look, man," we both said together, slowing to a stop and climbing off.

"I promise I didn't believe it." Sami dropped his bike, and I did too. "I was just checking. You know . . . after what I did in Turkey with my dad's money . . . for the boats," said Sami.

"Yeah, and I told you off even then for trying to steal from your dad!" shouted Aadam, squaring up to Sami.

"Bro, they said they had proof," I said, rushing between Sami and Aadam. "They were carrying your rucksack and chucking money from it. It's obvious that Callum has something to do with this."

Aadam dropped his shoulders and looked down. "I wish I'd died in Syria. Then I wouldn't have to live like this." He swallowed. "Always scared of getting deported, always hiding and living in the shadows. Always scared someone will tell on me."

I put my hand on Aadam's shoulder, and Sami covered his face. It seemed he couldn't take this.

"Don't say that, my bro. We need you. Look how you came, and *you* stopped Sami from leaving."

Sami stepped forward, his face now close to Aadam's. "Yeah, if it weren't for you telling Ali to bring you guys to the airport, I'd have probably got on that plane and died trying to get back to Syria, or maybe even got arrested."

"Look how you're always cheering us up when we're down. You're the one that tells us to keep going." I cleared my throat. "And look how you thrash us at football. We'd have massive heads if it weren't for you." I smiled at him, and he managed to pull one side of his lips up slightly.

"You came here for a reason, akhi." Sami nudged Aadam. "You were meant to be my big brother. Remember when you told me I couldn't leave because I was your brother and you had no one without me? Well, I need you too."

Aadam's face softened and he swallowed.

My brain went into overload. We *had* to help him.

"Allah knows best." Aadam raised his hands in front of his face. "Ya rabb, please help me."

"Ameen," Sami and I both said together. My voice croaked, trying to push back the uncomfortable lump in my throat. This was just an impossible situation for him to be in.

"Look, Aadam, forget Callum and Mark's mum," I said. "We need to focus on your lawyer's fees. I've got an idea."

Sami and Aadam both stared at me.

"*We'll* raise money for your legal fees," I said.

Sami's eyes widened and Aadam's face lightened. "How?" he asked.

"What, like, with a lemonade stand?" Sami smirked.

"Yeah 'cause we're five years old, Sami!" I rolled my eyes. "Nah, sponsored star jumps!" I started doing jumping jacks on the spot.

Sami looked at me as if I had just landed from Mars. Aadam started doing star jumps. Well, at least I'd totally distracted him.

I stopped jumping. "What do we all love?" I panted.

"Uhh, burgers?" said Sami.

"No!" I laughed. Aadam too. "We all love football.

So, why don't we organize a charity football match to raise money for your fees?"

"That's a brilliant idea," said Aadam.

"I know." I grinned. But my grin dropped right away when I spotted someone familiar behind Aadam and Sami, coming towards the playground.

"What's up?" asked Sami, turning round.

I felt like I'd been zapped and frozen.

"Ali?"

"Huh?" My voice cracked. I glanced at the man, who was now looking back at someone behind him, and turned quickly to Sami.

"Errr . . . nothin'." I shifted my feet. "We should get going," I said, looking down so my face wasn't visible.

I hadn't seen him in the flesh in about eight years, but I swear that was my dad.

Why the cruddery was he *here*?

Chapter 6

The doorbell rang on Monday morning. Sunday had whizzed by with me picking up Ahmed from footy, then tidying our room and doing my homework. I hadn't told anyone about what'd happened. Ahmed would've probably celebrated that I got kicked out of Mark's house, and Mum would've shot out the door like a firework to confront Mark's mum. Nah, it was much better not to tell them.

"All right," I said to Sami, and turned to grab my schoolbag. "Mark said he'll meet us at school."

"He's not gonna get dropped off here after what happened on Saturday, I suppose," said Sami.

"Yeah, doubt it. Think his mum's gonna drop him off in the Range."

"Ooh, the Range!" said Sami.

"Yeah. We finally get to see it. Shame we can't get a lift in it too. He said she's gonna drop him off and pick him up as much as she can now she's got the car, but he'll still bring his bike and ride with us sometimes." I pulled the front door closed, and we headed to school.

As we got near the school gates, a white Range Rover with tinted windows pulled up a few cars ahead of us. The front passenger door opened, and Mark jumped out.

"Mark!" I shouted.

"Hey!" He smiled as he slammed the door.

The front passenger window lowered. Mark's mum leaned across the passenger seat, her face twisted. "Mark, you're not to hang around with this lot anymore, I told ya!"

Mark's cheeks went pink.

"I mean it!" she shouted.

"All right!" Mark put his hands in his pockets and walked off.

I locked eyes with Sami. How were we supposed to respond to that?

Mark's mum closed the passenger window, signaled, and pulled out onto the road. I guess we were just supposed to suck it up.

Mark waited for us at the gate, his face still bright red. He shifted awkwardly. "Oh man, I'm so sorry. I don't even know what to say to you."

"It's not your fault," I said.

"No, listen," he said, and pulled us both to the side under a tree where no one could hear us. "I'm not arguing with her right now 'cause like I told you the other day, it's the first time I've seen her happy since Dad died. She's wearing makeup, singing, happy—how she used to be. I just said yes to her when she said I couldn't hang out with you guys, but I'm gonna do what I want when she's not around, obvs."

"Why does she hate *us*, though?" Sami asked. "She's literally flipped."

"Yeah, 'cause she believes whatever Callum says. She said it's good he's got a 'firm sense of discipline' and she can't trust you two now 'cause you might've helped Aadam get the cash, when you were inside."

"Yeah, but he didn't steal it," I said, putting my hands in my trouser pockets. "And you *knew* where we were, all the time."

"Look, I know." Mark leaned in to us. "She's just angry 'cause she thought she could trust Aadam and listened to me about giving him a job, so she's taking it out on us all. But with all the bad stuff on the news about criminals pretending to be refugees and that, her and Callum just keep going on and on, and now they don't want me to hang around with anyone . . ."

"With brown skin?" I said. "RUDE." I kicked the patchy grass under my feet.

"I know, but for now I'm just gonna pretend to listen till Callum calms down. You've seen—he's a bit much when he's angry." He gripped his rucksack strap so tight, his knuckles whitened.

"Yeah, I get that," Sami said. "Aadam was scared too."

Mark dropped his shoulders and stared off into the distance at nothing in particular.

The school bell rang, and we all headed to the entrance. Mark seemed more upset than he was letting on. I didn't want to make it harder for him after all he'd been through with his mum. We could still be mates at school, away from his mum and her nasty boyfriend.

Nathan and his mates pushed through the mass of bodies heading towards school and slowed next to us. "Watch it, idiot!" He stomped on the toes of Mark's new black Jordans and looked back at us, grinning as he walked off, nudging Tom and his other mates.

"Oi!" Mark scowled at him.

"The doofus can't even pretend he did it by accident." Sami shook his head.

Mark checked his Jordans for scuffs.

"Why is Tom hanging out with him again?" I said. We hadn't seen Tom and Nathan together since Tom had stood up for us in football training a couple of weeks ago and told Nathan his nasty behavior towards us wasn't funny.

"He's probably been forced to," said Sami. "Must be hard to get away from him after being neighbors for so long."

"Yeah, true."

My phone buzzed in my pocket. I pulled it out, looking around to make sure no teachers could see me. It was Samira, my sister.

> S: Dad's back on the scene. He messaged me.

I froze. So it *was* him in the park on Saturday.

"Ali, you coming?" said Sami.

"Huh? Uhhh, you go, I'll see you in form room," I said, before stepping out of the way of the crowd walking through the doors. I had to message Samira back.

A: What did he say?

S: He said he's back in the area. He lost his job and the council moved him here. Mustafa's here too.

Mustafa, his other son too? Ugh. My heart sank to somewhere near my socks. It was okay to move on from Dad when I didn't have to see him every day. What would I even say to him if we came face-to-face?

Part of me wanted to lash out and tell him what I thought of him, but another part—the part I tried my best to ignore—wanted Dad to say sorry for not being there for most of my life and just be my dad again. I swallowed the lump forming in my throat, switched my phone off, and shoved it in my blazer pocket.

I looked at the last of the kids heading to their form rooms. Why did Dad never call? No birthday cards. Nothing. How could he just live with us for so long and then one day leave and forget about us?

Dad had named me Ali, which meant "exalted." It meant "the best," which I'd clearly never been, because he named *him* Mustafa, which meant "the chosen one." That made me . . . the rejected one.

I puffed out a huge sigh, slung my rucksack on my shoulder, and headed to form time.

I had my head down in maths, trying to figure out how to solve an equation, while Sami was huffing and puffing and still trying to get comfortable next to me. His elbow knocked into mine, and I glanced at him. His upper lip was moist from all the stress the equation was causing him. I chuckled and he looked up.

"What?"

"Nothin'," I said. "Never seen you concentrating so hard."

I grinned, totally distracted now and not really in the mood to go back to my maths. I looked around the class. Everyone had their head down. The sun was shining outside, and the Year Sevens were playing football on the field. They looked tiny, even smaller than we were this time last year. Samira said Year Sevens got smaller each year, and looking at this lot, she was right.

TRRRRRRRRIIIIINNNNNNNNNNNNNG-GGGGGGGG.

We all jumped.

The fire alarm.

Nice timing! I pushed my chair back and stood up to load my bag.

Sami grabbed his and shoved his things inside. "It's so loud, man," he said, frowning.

"Leave your things and everyone file out. Quickly," said Mrs. Justin.

We all squeezed out into the stuffy corridor and headed towards the nearest exit, everyone chatting and excited that we were getting time out of lessons.

The breeze hit me as we walked into the playground. "Aaah, cool air." I smiled as I walked to the Year Eight section and lined up behind my form.

Mark joined his form next to ours, and we fist-bumped. I did a double take as I spotted about five girls all standing in a line, doing each other's hair. One of them, I think her name was Elle, shouted to another girl, "Wanna join our hair train?"

She giggled, swiping her hair back. "Nah, I'm good!"

The Year Sevens started lining up on our other side. A boy in his PE kit dribbled a ball down the line and got in the queue. He did a couple of keepie-uppies and then turned to smile at his mate behind him, and I saw the keepie-uppie boy's face more clearly.

NO WAY.

Mustafa had already started at *my* school?

My actual half brother?

I'd never met him officially, just seen him once at a family wedding when he was in the women's hall with his mum, and then just the odd photo in random family posts on Instagram that my sister had shown me, but this was definitely him. It had to be.

He grabbed the ball and asked the kid in front of him to move forward so he could keep doing more keepie-uppies. Half the kids in his form shouted, "GO, GO, GO!" He managed twenty before his teacher told him off and took his ball.

I felt hate seethe through my veins—something I'd never experienced before.

He was cocky and popular. And he was good with a football.

I stared down at my hands, to make sure no one could see my face, and gulped down my sadness. No wonder Dad didn't want to see me. He had everything he needed with him.

The chosen one.

Chapter 7

The next day it felt like I saw Mustafa at every turn. I saw him at break, on my way into French, and in the corridors too. And every time I saw him, I felt like a fire had been lit inside my belly, burning everything up inside me. Why did he have to come here, of all places? To *my* school? Did Dad just want to rub it in more?

We all sat down at lunch, and I scooped some hot baked beans into my mouth. Mark had loaded double the food he usually bought on to his plate. I suppose he could afford it now, and he had a lifetime of food to make up for.

Mustafa walked past our table with his tray and a group of friends. I still couldn't believe he'd joined just this week and was *already* popular. Lucky him. He didn't acknowledge me, even though he glanced at our table. He had to know that I existed.

Maybe Dad had messaged Samira about Mustafa joining this school, to warn me to stay away from his precious son, and she didn't have the heart to tell me?

Mark groaned. I focused on him.

"What is it?" Sami asked, leaning over to catch a glimpse of Mark's phone.

Mark showed us his screen. It was a photo of an old cruddy man wearing a blue tie, standing in front of a massive poster. On the poster was a photo of loads of refugees, just like the shots they showed on the news, all of them brown, standing in a field in a long snaking line. The UK flag was pasted in the bottom left corner. The caption on the poster said:

BREAKING POINT

and then below it:

Control Our Borders

I raised my brows.

"He's so nasty," said Mark.

"Who? That old man?" Sami said, pointing at Mark's phone with his fork. "He needs help controlling his *racism*."

I laughed.

"Yeah 'course *he's* nasty, but no, I meant Callum. Do you see why I haven't pushed Mum about having you guys over? I mean, he shares stuff like *this* on our family WhatsApp group."

"You have a family WhatsApp group with him?" I said, taking a sip from my water bottle.

"Yeah, he set it up. As if he could be my 'family.' The idiot."

"Has he said anything more about Aadam?" I asked, scooping up some fries and beans.

"Nah. Think he's forgotten about him now." Mark put his phone back down next to his plate. "He seemed happy they'd recovered the money. And I don't wanna say anything in case he gets angry again and calls the police or something."

I sat up. "You know what?"

"What?" said Mark, sipping from his orange juice carton.

"Forget him and his stupid poster. Let's plan the

charity match so we can help an actual refugee stay safe in England."

Mark laughed. "Nice one! And Callum will hate it when he finds out, ha ha!" He took a bite of pizza.

"So shall we do five-a-side or the full eleven?" asked Sami.

I thought about it for a moment. Although five players would be easier to manage, a proper team of eleven would probably mean we'd raise more money.

Mark leaned in. "I reckon eleven-a-side . . . So, how are we gonna raise the money? Ask players to pay to play?"

"Nah, I think we'd charge for tickets to watch, right? Ali?" asked Sami.

Mustafa howled with laughter at the table next to ours. I couldn't help but look over and stare. How was he always having so much fun? He seemed so happy all the time. I suppose having your dad around meant you had less to worry about. Bet he didn't have to get any shopping in for his mum. I bet Dad did all of that. Bet his mum had no worries in the world either.

Sami and Mark jabbered on about the charity match, but I couldn't focus now. I wanted to hear what my so-called half brother was saying.

Sami nudged me and said something.

"Huh?"

"What's up?" he asked, staring at me. "You look sick."

I felt sick. That was true. But there was no way I could tell him why. How did I go from being a happy lad with my mates to this burning-up-inside one?

≡

It was football training after school, so I waited for Sami in our usual spot near the science labs. His teacher opened the lab door, and the pong of rotten eggs trickled out. They must've done the same stinky sulfur dioxide and hydrogen sulfide experiment we'd done in the morning. I fanned my nose—it was bad enough smelling it once, but twice was just criminal.

Sami bounced out of chemistry and looked around as if he was bursting to talk.

"Guess what?" he said.

"What?" We started walking down the corridor towards the changing rooms.

"Aadam messaged. He spoke to his mum. She's found his head teacher! And he's gonna try and get some proof to show Aadam went to his school!" Sami beamed. "And his mum's gonna send some photos of where she lives and maybe her injured leg too."

"Okay..." I wasn't sure why that would be any help to us, and then it clicked. "Oh, for his new refugee application?"

Sami nudged me. "Yeah! And we could use his mum's pics for the fundraiser too!"

"Oh right!" I said. "I get it now. To show everyone why he can't go back to Syria yet? Yeah, that'd be really good actually."

"Hurry up, ladies, we haven't got all day." Nathan the crudhead brushed past us, swinging his PE bag.

I rolled my eyes at Sami. Nathan might have stopped making racist comments since getting into trouble and Sami replacing him as team captain, but he was now finding other ways to have a go at us.

"What were we just talking about?" I asked.

"Forget it, man. We'll chat later. That idiot ruins everything."

I shrugged as we piled into the changing room and hung our bags on the hooks.

"Oi oi!" Mark burst in with a grin on his face.

"What you so happy about?" I said.

"Going to meet Grace after our *FIFA* marathon, innit."

"For a date?" Sami asked.

"Nah. Just as friends . . . for now." Mark held his shoulders back and pushed a hand through his curly blond hair proudly.

I laughed as I pulled out my football kit.

"She had a go at me 'cause we didn't meet up for footy practice in the park all of last week." Mark hung his bag and checked his phone.

"Now we're not coming to yours, we should go again after school," I said, tugging off my shoes.

Mark's phone buzzed, and his face went pale and looked nothing like it had a few seconds ago.

"Who's that from?" I asked, pulling on my shorts. "She canceled on you already?"

"It's my mum." Mark sat on the bench, his head low and shoulders drooped, as if he'd let in twenty goals in one game or something.

"What did she say? Is it bad?" asked Sami, shoving his school trousers into his bag.

"She said I can't come to yours after training . . ."

"Oh man! For real?"

"Yup. I told her as soon as Callum kicked you guys out that I was with you all the time you were at ours, and there was no way you'd have taken any money anyway. She knows!"

I wanted to tell him to have another word. But looking at the state of him I couldn't. He was struggling.

I glanced at Sami and he shrugged. "Just play with us online."

"Yeah, exactly. We'll still all be playing together." I lightly punched Mark on the shoulder but he stayed droopy. "I'm gonna go warm up, yeah? You comin'?" I headed to the door.

"Yeah." Mark sighed and started taking his blazer off.

Leo pulled the door open; he looked so much taller, because he'd gelled his spiky brown hair up. I rushed through the door, then stopped.

Mustafa was coming out of the other changing room, wearing his school football kit.

I turned on my heel and went back into the changing room.

"Aaaaaaaaaaagh! AHMED!"

Sami and I walked into my house to hear my sister screaming at my little brother. I dropped my schoolbag next to my shoes and turned to Sami, putting my finger to my lips. He stopped where he was next to the front door, and I crept to the doorway of the front room.

"Why did you use my hairbrush?" Samira screeched.

"I never!" Ahmed said, looking up from his *Minecraft* game. "I don't even use a brush! I don't care about hair, like you!" He frowned and started playing again.

Samira stormed towards the door and stopped as soon as she saw me, with my perfectly styled brush-up. She pointed at my hair. "YOU CAME IN MY ROOM AND YOU USED MY HAIRBRUSH!"

"Well duh—this hair doesn't style itself, you know."

"I'm gonna kill you!" She came for me, and I dodged her so she fell through the doorway into the hall. Sami looked stunned and Samira blushed, clearly embarrassed that anyone outside our family had heard the "real" her.

"I couldn't find mine," I said. "What's the problem, anyway? It's not like I brushed the carpet with it. Just my hair." I shrugged.

She stomped upstairs, giving me evils through the spindles on the banister on the way up.

"Thanks!" I said to Sami.

"What for?" he whispered.

"Well if you weren't here, she'd have charged right back at me!"

Sami laughed and followed me into the front room. I grabbed Ahmed's controller and handed it to Sami.

"Oi! I was playin'," said Ahmed.

"Yeah, and now you ain't," I said. Ahmed's little eleven-year-old body bobbed up as I sank into our old three-seater sofa.

"Let him play with us, man." Sami handed the controller back to Ahmed and squeezed in next to him, nudging him with his elbow. "Wish I had a little brother to play with."

"All right, you two play," I said. "I'm gonna snooze." While Sami and Ahmed started a *FIFA* game, I put my head back on the sofa and closed my eyes. I actually had two brothers. One proper and one half. And the half brother had just turned up at school and settled in as if he was always meant to be there—a part of my life.

I peeked at Ahmed from the corner of my eye and wondered if he'd feel the way I did about Mustafa. Did Ahmed even remember Dad? He was a toddler when Dad left. Maybe he wouldn't care.

Ahmed squawked as Sami tackled him in the game.

I wasn't going to say anything about Dad and risk upsetting Ahmed. I didn't want him to feel like the same ocean had taken over inside his body and was crashing against his whole chest all the time too. Plus, I wouldn't know what to do if he cried and told me he missed Dad. I couldn't show him it affected me. I had to be the stronger one—his older brother who could handle anything. Nope, there was no point ruining Ahmed's life too.

Chapter 8

If Mark wasn't allowed to hang out at mine, we were going to make sure we would hang out together somehow. And we weren't going to give up our footy time just because Mark's mum and her boyfriend all of a sudden hated us.

The next day after school we all went to the park to play football, just like we'd been doing before Mark had moved into his mansion.

Grace was already at the park, waiting with two friends from her school. I squinted in the sun as Mark walked over and they chatted. Grace tucked a strand of hair behind her ear, then tied the rest up into a ponytail. Mark's smile was probably visible from space. That boy could not hide how he felt if he tried.

I swung my bag off my shoulder and dropped it, ready to create a makeshift goal. Sami dropped his about seven meters away. His phone rang, and he pulled it out and started talking in Arabic. It must've been Aadam or his mum. His dad would be at work, and they usually spoke in English when he called.

"Aadam said he can't make it right now. He's just finishing up his shift at the factory, but he'll try and get here in half an hour."

"All right, that's cool," I said, watching Grace, who was already in the midfield position.

"What about Elijah and Leo? Are they coming?" asked Sami.

"Nah, not today," said Mark, getting in goal. "They've got some school thing."

One of Grace's mates was setting up the other goal. Looked like it was girls versus boys today. It was on. We'd have to thrash them, otherwise we'd never live it down.

About twenty minutes later, after a warm-up and some drills, I kicked off and passed the ball to Sami. He dribbled as fast as he could to avoid Grace, who was already coming up behind him. He booted the ball to get it away from her and raced towards it; she ran harder and they both shoulder-barged each other trying to take

it. Grace got the ball and turned, going on the attack.
She took a shot, but it went wide.

"Free kick!" I shouted.

She turned and frowned. Sami laughed, delighted
with my football regulations even in the absence of a
referee. I gave the cheesiest smile I could, just like in my
school photo.

Mark came out of goal and kicked the ball towards
Sami. Grace swooped in and got it. I gritted my teeth,
praying she'd miss. *Come on, miss it.*

It hit the rucksack goalpost. "YES!"

Grace glared at me and walked back to the middle
of our pitch. Sami looked over, grinning. Then he did
a double take and his eyes widened, so I turned to see
what he was looking at. Aadam was sitting on a bench
with his head hanging low. This wasn't like him.

"I'm kicking off!" shouted Grace.

I raised my hands above my head and said, "Just give
us five!" as I watched Sami walking over to Aadam.

"You giving up already?" said Mark, panting and
putting his hand on my shoulder.

"Let's take a break." I nodded toward Aadam.

"All right, but don't be too long," said Mark, jogging back to Grace.

I walked up the path, following Sami through a swarm of tiny flies, swatting them away from my face. Mark was now chatting to Grace and her mate Leonie. Good. Football was one thing, but I didn't want Grace to think she could just get into our business too.

"What's up, Aadam? Why you not joining?" asked Sami, sitting on the wooden bench next to him.

Aadam didn't look up.

"You hurt?" I asked, squatting to see his face.

Sami locked eyes with me. Something was off.

"What is it?" Sami clutched Aadam's shoulder. "What happened?"

Aadam sighed. "I spoke with my lawyer. He needs a deposit from me before he can start writing my appeal and I don't have enough to pay him even that. And I just spoke to my mum . . ."

"What did she say?" asked Sami.

Aadam's eyes welled up. He swallowed and looked down at his hands, locking his dry fingers together and then unlocking them. "They've got no food or gas in Syria. She said they're eating . . . what do you call it . . . watercress and leaves now."

I glanced at Sami. "We're gonna speak to Mrs. Hack, our Director of Sport, tomorrow, don't worry,"

I said. "We'll get the fundraiser started and get your deposit."

Sami put his hand on Aadam's shoulder. "Let's speak to Baba today? I know you don't want to 'burden' him or whatever about the deposit, but we need to tell him."

Aadam nodded, his head still lowered.

I cleared my throat. "Let's go get a drink. I'm thirsty." I pointed at the shops across from the park. "Come on, what d'you want?" I asked Aadam, hoping to distract him a little.

"Nothing, but I will buy the paper. I need to read it before my English class tonight." Aadam put his hands in his pockets and followed us.

"Gonna get a drink. You want anything?" I shouted back at Mark and Grace. Grace was in the middle of saying something animatedly.

"Nah, I'm good!" he said.

"No, thanks, I've got this!" Grace shouted, waving her water bottle at us, and then carried on chatting.

We went to the small Co-op across the road. Aadam stopped at the front, picked up a parsley plant wrapped in plastic, and started examining it.

"What do you want that for?" I asked.

"It's half price. It will be perfect for tabbouleh tonight," he said, holding it up.

"You cooking again?" asked Sami, going past him into the shop.

"Yeah. It makes me happy!" said Aadam, taking the plant in with him.

"Would you ever be a chef?" I asked, following them inside.

"I think that's what I want to do. One day, I will open my own restaurant serving Syrian food, inshallah." Aadam smiled.

"I'll eat there every day!" I shouted after him as Aadam walked off, putting a thumb up at me.

I went straight to the fridges. Sami went to the chocolates aisle, and Aadam went to the magazines and newspapers.

I pulled the glass door open and shuddered as the cold air hit me. Clutching a bottle of Ribena, I went to find Aadam and Sami.

I stopped midstep as soon as I entered the magazine aisle.

Callum . . .

Mark's mum's boyfriend had cornered Aadam, who was trying to stop himself from falling back into the shelves. The parsley plant was on the floor, soil from it spilled all over the plastic it was wrapped in.

I wasn't sure what to do. If I shouted for help, Callum would see me and then might give Mark more grief at home. He'd do worse if I barged in to help Aadam. I looked around for Sami or a staff member. Anyone.

"Stay away from Mark, otherwise I'll make sure you get sent back to where you came from." Callum grimaced, his tanned face creased more than ever before.

Aadam swallowed and nodded. Callum pointed in Aadam's face to scare him, then pulled a property magazine off the shelf and walked down the aisle towards the pet food at the back.

"You okay?" I rushed over. "How did he know you were here?"

"I don't know. He picked up a magazine and then he saw me . . . I can't take risk," said Aadam, paler than I'd ever seen him.

"Can't take the risk for what?" asked Sami, holding a Kit Kat.

"Shhh!" I put my finger over my mouth. "Callum's here. He can't see us."

Sami's mouth dropped. "What happened?" he whispered.

"I can't play football with you no more . . ."

"Why?" Sami asked, edging closer to Aadam.

"He's gonna send me back to Syria if I go near Mark." Aadam sighed. "If he tells Home Office anything bad about me, I won't be able to even appeal, they will deport me." He looked around. "I have to go before he sees me again."

Sami screwed his face up. "He can't do that to you."

"That man is liar. He could make anything up," said Aadam, picking up the parsley plant and heading towards the end of the aisle with a newspaper.

"True," I said, following him. "Like he did with the money."

A cool breeze whooshed into the store as the automatic doors opened and Mark's mum walked in. I ducked down next to some shelves, and Sami and Aadam stepped back into the aisle behind me. I edged forward to peek, and Sami put his hand on my shoulder to spy with me. Callum picked up a bunch of flowers from a bucket near the entrance and handed the cashier a ten-pound note, nodding toward Mark's mum. He swaggered over to her, tucking the magazine under his arm while holding a four pack of beer, and handed her the bunch of red roses.

"Oh, for me?" Mark's mum's face lit up, and her eyes smiled too, not just her mouth.

"Anything for you." Callum grinned and then winked back at the cashier before putting his arm around Mark's mum and walking out the store.

The cashier smiled widely and stared after them, looking impressed by his Prince Charming performance.

I breathed out. "Let's give it a minute and then leave."

We walked to the cashier to pay for our stuff. I quickly handed over my drink and put my hand out for Sami's chocolate and Aadam's newspaper. "It's on me. We've got to be quick, come on."

Aadam sighed and handed it over. "I will pay you back."

"Yeah, me too," said Sami.

"What about the plant?" I asked Aadam.

"I don't feel like cooking anymore. I left it on a shelf."

Stupid Callum had ruined everything again.

I fumbled around my trouser pocket for a few

pound coins as Sami handed over his Kit Kat to the cashier.

Just as we'd paid, the automatic doors opened again and Mark swanned in. He smiled when he spotted us. "What's takin' you lot so long?"

Aadam glanced at me, Sami, and then at Mark. "Errr . . . ," he said, trying to squeeze past me at the counter. He looked like he'd been confronted by a ghost.

I stepped back so he could leave.

"I uhhh . . . I have to go." He gawped at Mark awkwardly. "I have to help Sami's dad. I can't play today, sorry." Aadam eyed Sami and then Mark again and rushed off.

Mark looked confused. "What were you lot gassing about?" he said, elbowing me as he joined us. He nodded toward the glass doors. "What is up with him? Come on, tell me. Grace isn't here. It's just me, look."

Sami scanned my face.

"I know something is going on. Aadam was acting well weird, and now you two are as well."

I unscrewed my bottle and put it to my mouth before taking a big breath. The smell of Ribena swam up my nostrils.

"What is it? Ali, you're annoying me now!"

I lowered the bottle for a second. "I think he should know," I said to Sami, and took a swig of drink.

"Know what?" said Mark, swatting a buzzing fly away.

"Yeah, you tell him," said Sami.

Mark's nostrils flared as I told him what Callum had said. He didn't say a word and instead rushed out of the Co-op. We ran after him, only to see him pick up his bag and storm out of the park.

Chapter 9

"*You took your time!*" said Sami as I sat down next to him at the computer in the school library the next day. "Where's Mark?" He scanned the room behind us.

"I dunno. Couldn't find him and his phone's off."

Sami was buzzing with excitement from head to toe. "Okay, so . . . this is what we'll do. Speak to Mrs. Hack about the charity football match after school. If she says yes, then we get a team together."

"Yeah, but are we gonna make enough money?"

"Well, I was thinking we could charge each player to play as well. So we'd be charging people to come and watch *and* players to play!"

"Yeah, all right," I said. "Sounds good. Actually, you know what? We could give each player a sponsorship form, so each one can raise money too. That'll make more."

"Yeah, that's a good idea! And with twenty-two players, we could make a fair bit towards the target!"

We fist-bumped just as the school bell went. Break was over.

"See you at lunch?" I said, scraping my chair back to stand.

"I've got a dentist appointment," said Sami, slinging his rucksack on his shoulder and heading towards the library door with me. "Mum said I have to go because it was so hard to find a dentist and if I miss it, I might not find another one who'll see me."

"Yeah, that happened to me, actually. They just boot you off the list if you don't go. All right, I'll see you in form time later then, yeah?"

Sami nodded, and we both split to head to our separate lessons.

≡

At lunch, I spotted one of our school football teammates in the lunch queue. "Hey, Leo!"

Leo nodded at me and made a space for me to join.

I grabbed a tray and looked at everyone behind him apologetically.

"Thanks," I said to the girl standing behind Leo as she let me in. I spotted Mustafa four kids down the line and swallowed. *Stay focused. Don't even think about him*, I told myself, and turned back to Leo. I put my tray down. "So, we're putting a special footy match together, eleven-a-side . . . ," I started, trying to figure out exactly how many inches his new spiky hairdo added to his height. At least two.

"For what?"

"To raise some money for Sami's brother, who needs our urgent help."

"Ah, right. Go on then," he said as he pushed his tray along the counter and picked up a knife, fork, and spoon.

"So we need eighteen more players. We'll do a spon- sored match instead of a sponsored run or whatever. Same thing but better." I grinned and picked up my knife and fork as Leo moved along.

"Errr, sausages and mash, please," he said to the dinner lady.

I couldn't have that, so I looked around him to see what the person in front of him had. Curry. Oh man, the curry in school just wasn't a proper curry. But that was the only option today. Ugh.

"So what do you think?" I asked as he moved on again.

"Yeah, sounds good. Not sure I'll get many sponsors though. I'm rubbish at that kind of thing. Plus, how is it gonna be something worth sponsoring if everyone knows we play all the time anyway?"

I chewed on my lip. "Don't worry, we'll figure that out," I said, putting my plate out to the dinner lady. She poured the runny curry all over some rice, and I thanked her.

"Leo!" Tom shouted from a table at the back of the hall. I'd have to try to chat to Tom at footy training, away from Nathan. Leo nodded at him, then looked at me. "See ya," he said before walking off.

This sponsorship idea wasn't a solid way of raising money. Leo was right: we played football all the time, and it wasn't like people were packing in to watch our matches. I'd struggle to get anyone to sponsor me too—except my mum and big sis. I sighed as I pulled out my lunch payment card and handed it to the cashier.

I went and found a table with spare chairs and

waited for Mark to turn up. Sami wasn't back from the dentist yet.

When Mark arrived, he just pushed his mash around his plate. His jaw was clenched, and he didn't say anything. What was up with him?

"You gonna eat that?" I said.

Mark looked up and pouted miserably, as if he had no energy to reply.

"Did Grace break up with you or something?" I asked.

"No!" he replied quickly. "You know we're just mates."

"Okaaay, then did your mum not give you your fifty pounds today?"

"Oi! No!" He rolled his eyes. "Mate, we used to eat cold beans out of a tin. I know she's spending loads, but she ain't lost it enough to be giving me fifty quid a day!"

"I know! Just wanted to liven you up . . . Worked, didn't it?"

He smiled, then sighed deeply.

I chewed some more of my rice and curry. "You ready to tell me, then?" I said.

"I can't take part in the charity match."

"You what?" I put my fork down.

"Yeah. You know I went home last night angry? I asked Callum why he'd threatened Aadam, but then the smart-ass changed the subject by asking how I knew about what he'd said to Aadam. Once Mum cottoned on I was playing footy with you lot when I'm banned from hanging out with you, she started shouting. I told them both I didn't care and I was gonna help Aadam with his legal fees by playing in a charity football match and they both said if I do that, I'll lose my phone and 'privileges.'"

"Whoa." I sat back in my chair. I wasn't sure what to say.

"Don't tell Sami. He's just gonna get upset."

"Yeah, but he'll figure it out when you're not there to play . . ."

"Oh yeah." Mark put his fork down and picked up his juice carton.

A clatter made me jump, and I looked up to see Mustafa sitting down at the table in front of us with his lunch tray. His plate was mostly clean. If he'd already eaten, was he moving to this table to get in my face?

"I'm going to get another drink. You want anything?" asked Mark.

"Nah, I'm good," I said as Mark walked off.

I watched Mustafa chatting to his mates. He made a joke, and they all laughed.

I swallowed back the choking feeling in my throat, sat up straight, and looked away. How could this one person make me feel so unworthy? He was born a year after me and a year before my little brother, Ahmed. That meant Dad was with Mustafa's mum way before he left us. How could he just get married again when he already had a whole family?

Mark plonked his drink on the table. I jumped and snapped out of my thoughts.

"I've made a decision," Mark said, sitting down. "I'm not gonna listen to them. Don't officially put me on the team sheet for the charity match, like on posters or whatever, but I'll be playing in goal."

"You sure?" I said, leaning forward with my arms on the table.

"Yeah. It's the least I can do for Aadam after how he's been treated."

Chapter 10

Sami and I went to the sports department as soon as the last bell went. The corridor was badly lit, as usual, and the smell of bleach filtered out of one of the toilets. I walked around the Wet Floor warning sign that the cleaner had left out. Maybe someone had an accident.

We stopped outside the Director of Sport's office. This felt like an instant replay. We'd been here about two weeks ago trying to tell Mr. Clarke, our football coach, about Nathan's racism. Mrs. Hack had just started her job, so we thought she wouldn't be able to help us, but we were wrong. Mr. Clarke had just told us to ignore Nathan's "banter," but Mrs. Hack made Nathan remove his captain's armband, made him say sorry, and then gave the armband to Sami. She was definitely the best person for us to go to about helping Aadam. Plus, we could always get her daughter, Grace, to back us up when they were at home if Mrs. Hack needed more persuading.

Sami gripped his rucksack strap nervously. "You ready?"

"Yeah," I said, then knocked on the door three times. "We better be quick before all the after-school-club kids turn up."

"Come in!" a muffled voice said.

Sami bit his lip and pushed the handle down to open the door. It smelled a whole lot nicer inside than out in the corridor, like someone had just sprayed air freshener.

Mrs. Hack sat with her back to us. Her desk faced the window and looked out at the field. As we stepped in, she turned.

"Oh, hello, you two!" She wheeled her chair back and spun it so she was facing us, her hands on her school-branded joggers. "I hope you've not had any more trouble from Nathan?"

My palms were sweaty, and I wiped them on my trousers. Why did I always get nervous talking to teachers?

"No, Miss," Sami said, looking as nervous as I felt. "We need your help with something."

"A charity football match," I piped up.

"Oh? Tell me more."

Sami gulped. "My older brother, Aadam . . . he's sixteen . . . he's not at this school, and, well, he's not my *official* brother but he lives with us. He—he's about to get deported . . . sent back to Syria . . . and he needs to appeal, but he doesn't have money to pay for a lawyer and so . . . we want to help him raise it."

A door slammed somewhere, and a bunch of kids rambled down the corridor. We both turned and stepped a little closer to Mrs. Hack.

"We want to organize a charity football match," I said, trying not to fidget. "And give all the players a sponsorship form to raise money. Just like a sponsored run . . . but better."

Mrs. Hack stood up. "I'm sorry, but I don't think we can help, boys. We aren't allowed to get involved in anything political."

Sami raised his brows.

"It's not politics, though, Miss," I said. "This is about a human being . . . It's actually about his human rights. He's a . . . What do you call it when someone comes here on their own, Sami?"

"Uhhh . . . an unaccompanied minor." Sami stepped in.

"He's just sixteen!" I splayed my hands.

Sami held his head higher. "And he'll be sent back to a place where people are eating watercress and leaves to survive right now. His mum's legs had to be amputated after a bombing and his dad was killed in it! He's like my brother, Mrs. Hack. How can I let him go back to that?"

"I'm really sorry to hear this." Mrs. Hack cleared her throat. "Okay, let me speak to Mrs. Greenwood. See what she says."

"Thank you, Miss," Sami and me said together.

Mrs. Hack gestured at the door to show us we could leave. We said bye and walked out.

"You know when we do those career surveys?" I asked Sami as he pushed the door leading into the playground. "I always put footballer but now I'm thinking we could be lawyers."

Sami looked at me. "Maybe we could be immigration lawyers for refugees."

"I'd charge a lot less than they're charging Aadam, that's for sure. I mean, how hard can it be to fill in a few forms?"

Mark was chatting with Elijah outside. Elijah had made the line going through his tapered afro thicker since I'd last seen him.

"Check out that line!" I said, swiping my hand across the side of my head.

Elijah laughed.

"How'd it go?" asked Mark.

Sami blew out. "Mrs. Hack said she has to ask Mrs. Greenwood 'cause it might be political."

"Oh man!" Mark pulled his water bottle out of the side of his bag.

"What would be political?" Elijah asked.

We told him about our plan.

"You could just do it at the park." Elijah shrugged.

"Yeah, could do," I said. "But it would be easier to do at school." I wouldn't know how we'd get everyone together, if everyone would get permission to come, and if anyone would even turn up. Nah. School was definitely the place to do it. We had to convince them somehow.

≡

I pushed the cool steel door handle into the burger place and held the door open for Sami and Mark. We'd decided to get something to eat before heading home, given that the food at school had been so manky today and our conversation with Mrs. Hack about the charity football match hadn't exactly gone as we'd expected. I handed Mark my two pounds and got us a table before any other school kids came in and it got too busy.

Sami went to the front with Mark and ordered his chicken burger and chips meal. A man in the kitchen scooped fries into a cardboard box, then added a steaming-hot fried chicken drumstick on top before closing the lid. Oh, that smelled good.

The cash register pinged open, and the takeaway guy said, "Have you not got anything smaller?"

I grinned. Mark's big notes drained all the change from shop cash registers.

"Uhh... no..." Mark searched around in his pockets looking for pound coins.

"It's okay, I'll get it," said Sami, handing two pounds to the takeaway guy. Mark handed him my two pounds too.

"Thanks, I'll pay you back in a bit."

Sami shrugged as if to say it didn't matter, even though I knew those two pounds were probably his lunch money for tomorrow. They both took their receipts and slid into the seats at our table.

Sami fiddled around with the saltshaker. "So, we already know Elijah's in, but I'm thinking we should speak to the rest of the team about the charity match at training tomorrow. See how many of them want to play. Then at least we have one team if Mrs. Greenwood says yes."

"Oh, I already spoke to Leo in the lunch queue today," I said, picking up the pepper shaker.

"Oh right, what did he say?" Sami leaned in.

"He said it sounded good. I'm worried Nathan will cause havoc though, when he finds out."

"He won't," said Mark. "He'll do anything that makes him look good to teachers so he can be captain again." His smile dropped as he looked out the window behind me.

I turned to see what he'd seen. Ugh. Nathan.

Shouldn't have talked about him. Seemed we'd somehow conjured him here.

"There he is!" said Mark. "Shall we prep him now, so we've got a chance of him being supportive tomorrow?"

"Nah, not now," said Sami, putting the saltshaker back in its tray next to the wall. "No one wants to talk to him outside of school. He'll ruin my burger, man."

Mark looked at me and we both laughed.

"True, I ain't doing anything to put me off my burger." I glanced back to check if Nathan was coming in. He said something to Tom, took a sip from his Coke bottle, screwed the lid back on, and walked off. Yeah, he wasn't going to come into a halal burger place—it was a bit of a surprise he'd even stood outside, to be honest.

"How's Aadam doing?" Mark asked Sami.

"He's all right. He's keeping his head down, studying for his English test at the community center, and Dad got him some extra shifts at the old factory he used to work at."

"I'm sorry about Callum."

"It's not your fault, Mark!" said Sami.

I sighed. "We're never gonna swim in that pool again, are we?"

"You will!" said Mark, sitting up. "I'm just not pushing it right now with Mum, but I'll find the right time."

The man behind the counter shouted a number, and we all checked our receipts.

"That's us," said Mark, sliding out of his seat and grabbing our receipts to hand over to the man.

"Burger time!" Sami rubbed his hands.

I got up to take the tray Mark was handing to me

and put it in front of Sami. "There, you first. Not gonna let anything get between you and your burger!"

Sami unwrapped his food and took a bite. He wasn't waiting for no one.

We stepped out of the burger place into the warm late-afternoon sun. I squinted at the parade of shops. "I've just got to go and get some milk for my mum before we head home."

Sami nodded.

A couple of boys wearing football shirts laughed out loud like a pack of hyenas. We all stopped. They were standing next to a bright red Porsche 911 convertible with two turbo exhausts. It had its top down and expensive-looking beige leather seats. The car had been polished, and it looked like it had just come out of a showroom.

It wasn't often you'd get a car like this parked up on the parade, but when you did, you couldn't help but stare.

Sami elbowed me and nodded at the boys. One of the boys in full club kit had a key in his hands, and the other boy was egging him on. "Go on! Just do it quickly before he comes out!"

Do what?

"They're gonna key that Porsche!" Mark shouted.

"Oi!" We all yelled and ran towards the boys.

The ginger lad with the key in his hand stepped back, but the other one, who was wearing a cap, grabbed the key and stretched towards the Porsche.

I raced to him. "You better not!" I shouted.

"What you gonna do? Fight me?" The boy with the cap pushed his chest out and squared up to me.

"And are you then gonna fight the police too?" said a man's voice from behind me.

The cap boy's eyes almost popped out of his head. He gulped and ran off down the street.

I turned to see Sami and Mark standing with their mouths gaping. My mouth soon followed.

It was David Mora.

One of the best goalkeepers in Premier League history!

Oh my Wotsits.

Chapter 11

"*Thanks for that!*" David put his hand out.

I shook it, feeling as if I was having an out-of-body experience. Should I ever wash my hand? Should I sell it?!

He had his hair tied back in a tiny ponytail with his head shaved underneath it. His ashy-brown goatee glistened in the sun. Maybe he used that beard oil I kept seeing ads for on YouTube.

"You lot have just saved me a lot of stress." He opened his Porsche door and tossed a gallon of milk in the passenger seat, before sliding in behind the leather steering wheel. "I take it you're not rival fans like those two clowns trying to key my car?" He glanced in his rearview mirror.

"Never!" Sami said, grinning. "I have a poster of you and the team up on my bedroom wall!"

"Yep, watch all the matches and got all the merch too," said Mark.

"Oh, nice. Well maybe you can come and watch a home game sometime as a thanks from me?"

"That would be AMAZING, David . . . errr . . . Mr. Mora!" said Sami, and we all grinned at each other.

"Oh, you can call me David!" His phone rang. "Hold on." He put his hand up at us to tell us to wait and took the call. About five seconds after he answered, he said, "All right, I'm on my way." He looked at us, his brow creased. "Sorry, I'm gonna have to go. My dog's run off. Think he got out through the gate as I left. I've got to go find him!" He signaled, pulled out of his parking spot, and sped off down the road, his engine roaring.

"Oh man! We almost had tickets to an actual game!" Sami flapped his arms by his side.

"Gutted," I said.

Mark shrugged. "Mate, we just saved David Mora's car from being keyed. We are heroes."

"True. But I already knew we were." I grinned.

An old, banged-up maroon car with its windows

down pulled up into the spot David's car had been in, its exhaust spluttering.

As soon as I saw who was driving it, my stomach dived as if I was on a roller coaster drop. I didn't know if I should run back inside the burger place or put my hood on.

My dad scrambled out of the car and closed the thin, rickety door. He looked at us all, then did a double take, walking up to me slowly as if I was an interesting exhibit in a museum.

"Ali?" he said. He was wearing a black leather jacket. His hair was gelled up at the front, even though he'd started going bald on the top of his head.

"Uhhh . . . yeah. Salaam."

He smiled widely. "You look just like my Mustafa!"

Heat like fire flushed through my body. *His* Mustafa?! I clenched my teeth. He didn't even see me as his son. As if there was only *one* of us. When actually, he had three other kids.

"I thought it was him and was about to tell him off for hanging out on the street." He laughed.

"We're not hanging out here," I snapped, glancing at Sami and Mark, who looked like they wanted to run away. "I'm just gonna get some milk for my mum and then we're going home."

"Oh, okay . . . Well, come round sometime," he said.

How could he have the nerve to invite me over as if we were old family friends who had just bumped into each other? He sounded as insincere as Mum's friends did when they'd see us at the mosque on Eid. No one ever meant it when they said "come round," really.

I wanted to say, "I don't know where you live," but I stayed quiet.

He tugged on his jacket then forced a smile. "Give me your number and I'll text you the address."

I recited my number to him slowly.

My dad punched it into his phone, smiling at Sami and Mark—who at this point would've blended into the wall if their clothes had matched—and walked off towards the convenience store as if he'd just taken the number off some random person and not his long-lost son.

My phone buzzed. He'd already texted. I swiped on the notification:

> **D:** my number

Then he sent another text giving me his address.

That was it. I wasn't even worth an "It was good to see you." I was really nothing to him. Nobody.

Sami and Mark stared at me, waiting for me to say something.

I shrugged and put my phone in my pocket. I didn't want to tell them it was my dad.

They didn't say a word on the way home. It was as if they were respecting a mourning person's grief at a funeral.

But I was grateful, because I really didn't want to chat as if everything was normal right now. I had so many things going around my head. Should I answer Dad if he called me? Should I tell Samira and Ahmed I'd met him and got his number? And what about Mum? How would she feel if I did talk to Dad? I mean, he'd let her down big-time. Would I be disloyal to her to even admit that I wished he'd been around, especially after everything she'd done for us?

She'd struggled on her own and raised us, while he was having the time of his life with his wife and "chosen" son. Nah, there was no way I could take this further. I didn't even know why I'd wasted so much of my time thinking about the man.

The next day, I was walking out of a lesson, putting my chemistry book in my bag, when I knocked into someone.

"Sorry!" said the person I'd bumped into, and I looked up to say, "It's all right," but I didn't get a chance. Mustafa looked at me blankly and walked off. As if he didn't know who I was.

THE RUDE CRUDHEAD!

"Ali!" Mark tapped my arm. "Is Sami already in the library?"

"Uhh . . . I think so. I didn't have a lesson with him."

As soon as we stepped into the library, Sami stood up. "Come on! I've got a mega update!"

"What is it?" I asked, trying to look interested while looking around for Mustafa. Why had he just walked off? So it wasn't just Dad who thought Mustafa was better than me—*he* thought he was better than me too. I bet Dad and Mustafa sat there laughing at the loser family he left behind. I breathed out.

"SO," said Sami. "Mrs. Hack saw me after PE and we've got a date!" Sami grinned.

"A date for what?" I asked.

"Oh my God, Ali!" said Mark. "Where's your brain at?" He tapped my head. "The charity football match, obviously."

"Oh, yeah!" I forced myself to smile. I turned to the library door when I heard it open. It was a boy in Year Nine. Not Mustafa. I just couldn't focus.

"Mrs. Greenwood said yes!" Sami continued. "She said we can hold it at the end of the month, so we haven't got long—it's just three weeks away! She's gonna call my dad in to go through things properly but she said we can start promoting it. So let's plan the poster now!" Sami's eyes were sparkling, but right then, I couldn't imagine what being that excited or happy even felt like.

The computers were all being used, so Mark went to the printer and came back with a sheet of blank paper. Sami pulled out his pencil case from his bag while I sat with my arms folded on one of the tables.

Sami started writing the title in his fancy curly-wurly handwriting.

"Draw a net here . . . and a ball about here," said Mark, pointing at parts of the paper.

I put my head on my arms. What was the point of trying? I'd probably mess things up for Aadam anyway. Dad clearly didn't think I was good enough for any-thing, and he was probably right.

"What's up with you?" asked Mark.

"Nothin'. I've got a headache," I lied.

"All right, we'll get this done and then we can head to lunch, yeah?" said Mark.

"Yeah," I said, feeling as if someone had put a pin in my body and drained the air out of me like a limp balloon.

Chapter 12

Later that day, after school, Sami stood in the changing rooms with his head high and his shoulders back. He had his serious team-captain face on and was checking if everyone had their shin pads before training started.

I looked at him proudly. He was made for this, and it was amazing to see him go from losing all his confidence to being the leader he was always meant to be. Even though Nathan's racism and bullying had made our lives on the team unbearable last month, it had worked out, because Sami would never have got a chance to step up and show his skills otherwise.

I threw my school shirt into my kit bag and pulled out my football top. Everyone was here except for Nathan. He turned up at the last minute a lot now that he wasn't captain. I think it was because he really couldn't handle Sami telling him what to do.

Sami cleared his throat. I glanced up at him as I pulled my shorts up over my knees, avoiding Leo's deodorant spray wafting all around me. I'd told Sami he should speak to the team when he'd asked me to do it. He was Aadam's family, and he was also captain. Plus I didn't want to mess things up. I wasn't gonna be a lawyer for anyone. I don't know why I ever thought I would be good enough.

"Uhhh . . . we're doing a charity football match to raise some money for my . . . older brother. He— he needs urgent money to stop the government from sending him back to Syria, where he'll be in danger and probably be forced to fight in the war."

We'd agreed it was just easier to say "older brother" than to explain Aadam's real situation to everyone.

Sami looked at all of us. I folded my arms and nodded to encourage him to carry on.

"So, uhhh . . . we spoke to Mrs. Hack and she said we can hold it here in three weeks. We were thinking of doing a sponsored match, so we'll give you a form and you raise as much as you can to play. Who's in?" He searched all our faces, and I put my hand up. Mark too, then Elijah and Leo, who looked at me and nodded. I think he was acknowledging our earlier conversation. Within seconds, everyone had their hands up.

"Awesome!" Sami said. He high-fived everyone, one after the other. "We'll get the sponsor sheets ready for Monday. But you can start asking people over the weekend."

"There's also gonna be tickets for spectators, to help us raise more money," added Mark. "So let people know if you can." He sat on the bench to tie his laces.

"I'll bring my whole fam!" Elijah said, heading to the door. He always got ready first. Probably because he was used to getting out of the changing room as fast as he could when Nathan was captain.

Where was Nathan? He was cutting it close.

"How many tickets can we sell?" asked Leo.

"Uhhh . . ." Sami looked my way.

I shrugged. "As many as you want, really."

"Yeah, we can fit loads of people on the field around the pitch, so I don't think we have to worry," Sami said as he adjusted his shin pads.

"Yeah, exactly," I said, looking at Sami.

"But maybe we should check with Mrs. Hack first?" said Sami.

"I'm sure she'll say the same," said Mark.

Everyone started chatting to each other, and Elijah pulled the door open and left. I guess they were done talking about the charity match.

I squeezed Sami's shoulder and he smiled.

"Let's go," said Mark. His hand was on the door handle, when Nathan pushed the door in, and Mark with it. "Hey!" Mark shouted.

Nathan shrugged and barged in using his kit bag as if it was a battering ram. I sidestepped, giving him a look, and he missed me.

Mark gave Nathan evils and walked out. Sami swallowed. It looked like he was wondering if he should speak to Nathan. I caught Sami's attention and shook my head. He followed me out of the changing rooms.

"Leave him for now," I said. "He's obviously in a mood."

"Yeah." Sami tapped me on my arm. "I'll just go chat to Mr. Clarke before we start."

I looked over as Sami jogged off. Mr. Clarke was talking to Mustafa.

Ugh. He even had to get in there with my football coach. What was he even saying?

I recalled Mustafa's face earlier today when I'd bumped into him. He'd acted like I didn't exist. Totally unaware of the impact *his* existence had on my life. I wished he hadn't moved here. Why did he have to come and ruin everything?

That night, Mum picked up my plate from in front of me. "Ali, did something happen at school? You haven't eaten properly."

"Not that hungry," I said, shrugging.

Ahmed shoveled the last of the chicken pasta into his mouth and got up, scraping his chair back. Mum picked up his plate, and Ahmed washed his hands and rushed out of the kitchen—probably to finish the game he'd paused.

"You need to eat, beta."

"No, Mum. I don't need to eat twenty parathas and seventy-five samosas every day. Not everything's about food, you know. This isn't Pakistan."

Mum blinked hard and raised an eyebrow. Oh man. I'd hurt her. She showed she cared with food and now I'd just had a go at her about it.

"Is this about your dad moving back? Have you seen him?"

I nodded. So she knew he was back too.

"When? Where?" She closed the oven door, shutting off the heat and garlic-bread smell coming from it.

"Saw him yesterday after school when I went to get milk."

"What did he say?"

"Nothin' . . . just texted me his number and told me to go round."

"Do you want to?"

"No." I stared at my balled-up fists on the table.

"You've not been yourself for a good few days now. I wasn't sure if you knew about your dad, but Samira said today that she told you he'd moved back here. I should've mentioned it before. I just didn't know how." She sat opposite me and put her mug of tea on the dining table. "Did Samira tell you about his son starting at your school? Have you seen him?"

I nodded.

"Do you want to talk about it?"

I shrugged.

She took a sip of her tea, and there was a long silence while she stared at me. I wanted to get up and leave, but for some reason my legs wouldn't budge.

"You were only five when he left," she said, and I looked up.

"Why did he leave?" I asked.

Mum sighed deeply. "He was already in love. With someone else, I mean . . . before we got married."

"Who?"

"The woman he's married to now. He was young and in a relationship with her, basically messing around, and your dada thought if he got his 'wild son' married, he'd settle down and behave. So, they asked me, and I obviously didn't know about his 'first love.'" She put the "first love" in air quotes.

"So we got married and had Samira and then you, but he was barely home by the time I got pregnant with Ahmed because he'd already done his nikah with her but hadn't told me."

"Nikah?"

"They had an Islamic marriage ceremony in a mosque somewhere . . . I shouldn't have been surprised when I came home one day from the school pickup to find he'd packed all his stuff and left."

"What, he didn't even tell you?" I sipped some orange juice from my cup.

"No."

"So that's why you were always crying."

"Yeah . . . it wasn't easy. I didn't know how I'd bring you all up by myself. Three kids is . . . a lot."

"You did it though, Mum. You raised us all by yourself. You didn't need him." I swallowed back the choking feeling rising in my throat. Mum didn't need him—she was fine. But *we* did when we were little. Not that he cared.

"I know you struggled when he left, beta." She put her hand on my arm. "What are you feeling?"

I pulled my arm away. "I'm feeling nothing, because he means nothing to me. I don't even know him."

I pushed my chair back and walked out of the kitchen. I stopped outside the front room, considering if I should play a game with Ahmed to get rid of the ache in my chest, but instead I headed upstairs, lay on my bed, and put my headphones in, playing the angriest rap I could find on my playlist.

Chapter 13

The doorbell rang on Monday morning, and I ran to open the door. Sami stood outside with one hand on his bike saddle and the other in his pocket. Not chirpy like he had been last week.

"What's up with you?" I said, turning to grab my schoolbag and blazer.

Sami sighed and turned from the door to head to school. He really wasn't chatty today.

"Oi, Sami, what happened, man?" I pulled on my shoes and stepped outside, blinking as the sunlight hit my eyes.

Sami stopped wheeling his bike and waited for me to join him. "We haven't raised any money for the charity match. And Aadam *has* to send in his appeal by the end of this week. That's the deadline."

"We need more teams. Two teams of eleven players were never gonna raise enough money."

"Yeah, but we literally haven't raised even a penny yet." Sami adjusted his rucksack strap, his head low.

"Let's chat to Elijah and Leo at park footy today." I couldn't stand seeing him like this. "See if we can get any other ideas." I grabbed my bike from behind our side gate and nudged him to get us walking. "I asked my sis to sponsor me, and I've got some." I tried to sound positive, but there was no way I was gonna tell him Samira put down 50p. Just 50p! I reckon she did that 'cause it was me. If I asked Sami to ask her to sponsor him, she'd probably give him a tenner. Maybe I'd do that, just to make sure I squeezed more out of her.

As we got through the school gates, I spotted Tom and Nathan chatting to some of the school football team by the bike racks.

"Oi! Tom!" I shouted, glancing at Sami as we both made our way to him, wheeling our bikes.

"What?" Nathan snarled, and put his hands in his pockets. Great. He was getting involved.

I went over to Tom and put a U-lock around the frame of my bike, securing it to a rack. "About the charity football match . . ." I stood up. "We were thinking of opening it up to more people 'cause two teams getting sponsored is never gonna raise enough money. Not everyone can get sponsors—"

Nathan laughed, and I stopped talking to figure out what he found so funny.

"You guys are so dense. We play all the time anyway, so why would we pay to play?"

"You're not paying to play. You're supposed to get sponsored. It's to help my brother," said Sami, standing next to me after securing his bike.

"Yeah, and?" Nathan rolled his eyes. "Why would anyone wanna pay to help a 'poor boy from Syria'?" He made air quotes and said the last part in a mocking voice.

"You're just salty because you're not captain anymore," I said.

Nathan pushed me and I skidded, stopping myself from falling. I lunged at him but froze when I felt lots of eyes on me. I decided to save myself from getting in trouble.

"Come on, let's go." I stared down Nathan and pulled Sami away.

Sami drooped his head. "He's right, though. Why would anyone? Why'd we even think this was gonna work?"

As much as I hated thinking this, Nathan was right. No one was gonna care about helping a random teen-ager from Syria.

After a moment, Sami said, "Let's just cancel it so we don't look like fools, and find another way to help Aadam."

I pulled my slipping rucksack strap back onto my shoulder. "Look, man, we just need to find something more interesting to do. Maybe a penalty shoot-out or something? Something that more kids, even the ones that don't play, can get involved in, yeah? And doesn't necessarily have to involve the whole team, or Nathan."

"Yeah, maybe." But Sami didn't seem convinced.

≡

After school, we went to the park with Leo and Elijah for a kickabout. I felt much better than I had all weekend. Just me, the ball, and my boys. The way it used to be. Away from the possibility of bumping into Mustafa.

Elijah kicked off, and within minutes, Sami scored because Mark spotted Grace and didn't follow the ball. We all eye-rolled at each other.

"Mark, just go and have a chat!" Leo shouted, pointing to Grace and signaling a time-out.

"Yeah, just go. We'll talk about the charity match," I said, heading towards Elijah, Leo, and Sami.

We all sat on the grass. "So we're thinking of doing a penalty shoot-out instead of a match to raise money for Aadam. What do you think?" I said, looking at Sami and nodding to get him talking.

"You'll have to make sure Grace ain't around if you want Mark to stay in goal, otherwise we'll all score!" Elijah grinned and we all laughed. "Sounds good, though," he added.

"Yeah, better than that sponsorship thing," said Leo, pushing his brown mop off his face. He'd not spiked his hair up today, and he looked so different. More my height. "What do we have to do? Pay per penalty kick?"

"Yeah, I think that would work," said Sami, squinting as the afternoon sun blinded us.

My brain pinged. We could have prizes to get more people involved. "Yeah, and there'll be a big prize for the person who scores the most goals." I lay back on the warm grass, letting the sun do its thing on my face. "If we can get at least one hundred people from our year to pay three pounds for three penalties, we'll have three hundred pounds from just our year. And that's taking out around eighty people who won't wanna take part."

"And if we can get all the year groups to do it, we might raise fifteen hundred pounds!" Sami's voice was high and excited.

"What you lot talking about?" It was Mark, with Grace just behind him.

I sat up.

"More like, what have *you* been talking about?" Elijah winked twice.

Mark blushed and Grace scowled before sitting down with us. Sami filled them in.

"Penalties sound good! I heard Mum talking to your head teacher about Aadam last night." Grace pulled out a few blades of grass. "She said she's well impressed with how you want to do this."

"For real?" Sami said.

"Seriously?" I said at the same time.

"Yep." Grace blew the blades of grass into the warm breeze.

"I want to help too," she said. "I know it'll be at your school, but maybe I could help sell tickets at mine?"

"Yeah, that would be awesome," said Sami, grinning.

"Cool. I'll ask some mates too." Grace jumped up to grab the ball. "Come on, are we playing or not?"

"Let's do penalties!" said Leo.

"Yeah, all right," I said.

After the park, we rode our bikes to Mark's to drop him home. It was a warm evening, and me and Sami didn't feel like going home yet.

As we entered Mark's pretty, tree-lined road, Sami stopped. "Shall we head back?"

"Why, 'cause Callum might see us?" I said quietly, as Mark stopped riding and looked back at us.

"Yeah."

"You heading off?" shouted Mark. "What about your chemistry book? Mum got me a new one; you can have yours back."

"I'm coming," I said, nodding at Sami to say, "Come on."

"All right, I'll just run in and get it. You guys wait somewhere close to the drive."

We all stopped outside Mark's big gates and made

sure we weren't anywhere near the gate buzzer and camera.

Mark had started tapping in the entry code when his neighbor's gate clacked and started opening. We all turned, and a bright red Porsche 911 drove out with its top down, the engine purring like a happy cat.

Oh. My. God.

David Mora was Mark's neighbor?

Chapter 14

My jaw was on the floor for the second time in a week. Sami's and Mark's hung open too.

My hand involuntarily waved, without me even thinking about it, and my mouth broke out into what must've been a really cheesy grin. I couldn't help it!

David stopped his car and smiled.

NO WAY!

"Which one of you lives next door?" He looked at each of us. "I've got a couple of footballs to return." Then his face changed. "Didn't I meet you the other day outside the Co-op in Stockport?"

"Yeah, that was us!" Sami said.

"Don't worry, I made sure my dog's in the house and not following me out today." David smiled.

"Uhhh . . . I'm the one who lives next door." Mark leaned his bike on the wall next to the gate and turned to the car.

My mind was whirring. Why would we all of a sudden be chatting to a famous footballer for the second time in a week? This was fate. I had to make the most of this moment.

"Can I ask you somethin'?" I said. I'm not sure why, but I had a good feeling.

"Yeah, go for it," said David.

I stepped off my bike and held on to the handles. "Uhh . . . we're raising money for Sami's brother, who's about to be deported to Syria." I pointed at Sami. "Because they think he's an adult and he doesn't have proof he's from there 'cause he lost all his papers. He's only sixteen and it's not safe for him to go back as there's still a war happening. So we're planning a charity football match to raise funds for a lawyer to help him."

"Or maybe a penalty shoot-out," Sami chipped in. I'd forgotten we'd just changed the plan.

"You want me to donate towards it?"

"Uhhh . . . you could!" I said quickly. "But it would be *so* amazing if you could join us as our goalkeeper?

We'd get *loads* of people wanting to take part and donate and because of you we might even be able to get more attention in school and raise awareness about how hard it is to come as a refugee and stay in England too."

"Well, I owe you one for stopping those boys from keying my car . . . but I'm afraid I can't spare the time at the moment. It's not the end of the season for a couple of weeks."

"But that's perfect," said Sami. "The shoot-out's at the end of May!"

"Ah, then you'll have caught me after the season will have ended and I'll finally have some free time." David grinned.

"YESSSS!" said Mark, punching the air.

"A penalty shoot-out is perfect. Let's do it." He glanced at his phone. "Let me know the exact date, who's organizing it, and I'll be there."

"It's on Friday, twenty-seventh May, at our school. In just under three weeks," said Sami.

"Oh man, we can't thank you enough!" I said.

"Okay, just post the details—venue and time and whatever else—through my letterbox, and I'll see you then." David smiled, then looked left and right and drove off.

"DID THAT JUST HAPPEN?" shouted Sami.

"YEAAAAHHH!" I screamed.

We all ran into a huddle and patted each other's backs. Sami's eyes sparkled, and Mark started jumping on the spot. My face hurt from how hard I was grinning.

"Okay, so we have to make some posters with David on them," Sami practically squealed, gripping both my and Mark's shoulders. "We should call it a *VIP* penalty shoot-out fundraiser!"

"Everyone's gonna go wild when they find out!" I jumped on the spot some more.

Mark's phone beeped, and he pulled it out of his pocket. "Let's go make the posters at mine!" said Mark, grabbing his bike from against the wall.

"Seriously?" I said.

"What about Callum and your mum?" asked Sami, who wasn't grinning anymore.

"They're out. My mum messaged earlier saying she'd left some food in the oven for me, but I only just saw it now 'cause Grace messaged. We'll have it done in half an hour! They won't be back till after that, for sure."

I put my hands in my pockets. "Yeah, go on then."

Sami looked at me and raised his brows.

"What?" I said.

Sami leaned in close. "You sure we should do this?"

"Well, we haven't got long to promote it now and we need to get some posters out. Be good to make a start today."

"We can also make a start online. We don't have to do it in the house where Callum lives . . ."

An engine roared on the main road, and my ears pricked. I was just about to answer Sami, when his face changed.

"OI!"

I turned to see who it was.

Oh no.

Callum was driving the Range Rover and had the front passenger window down. He stopped in the middle of the road, put one hand on the steering wheel, and leaned over Mark's mum. His face grew red as he yelled at us, "What the hell are you two doing here? I told you I don't wanna see you again, didn't I?"

From the corner of my eye I saw Sami step back.

"If you don't leave now, I won't be responsible for what I do to ya!" He opened his door, and his shoulders emerged as he got out.

Mark's eyes were wide. He was obviously intim-idated by Callum. And I didn't want him to get into more trouble.

I nodded at Sami. We both climbed onto our bikes. I put my feet on the pedals and we raced off.

Chapter 15

That evening, I jumped onto the sofa with a couple of cookies in my hand. I shoved one into my mouth. David Mora knew who we were, and he was going to help us!

I messaged Sami.

A: Did you tell Aadam about David?

S: Yeah! You should've seen his face.

A:

S: Actually

A WhatsApp video call came in. It was Sami. I swiped and saw Aadam's face. He was close to the screen and was grinning so wide, he looked like a different person.

"Aadam! My bro!"

"I can't believe David Mora is going to help me! Akhi, this is the best day ever. Thank you for asking him!"

"I dunno what made me ask, man. But I had a good feeling . . . It was fate."

"Yes! Qadr. It was Qadr of Allah."

I smiled. I hadn't seen Aadam this happy, ever. Not even on the football pitch when he was thrashing us.

"We're gonna get the posters up tomorrow and hopefully raise some money for your deposit this week."

Mum came in with a mug of tea and a cookie and sat on the sofa. I pulled my legs back to make more room for her.

"Yes, I speak with Sami's dad. He is going to help with the deposit too. And my friends at unaccompanied minor center also help me with the little savings they have."

"Ah, cool! That's good."

"Okay, akhi, I have to go now. I need to finish

making my baklawa before my English class at community center at seven o'clock. I can't be late."

"All right, bro. Enjoy. See you later."

Sami came on. "I'll chat to you tomorrow. We gotta eat." He faced the camera to the floor and showed me a large plastic mat with dinner plates and rice and other dishes full of food on it. Then he showed Aadam standing in the kitchen pouring a clear liquid over a tray of what looked like cooked pastry.

"In a bit, Sami." I put the other cookie in my mouth and hung up, putting my phone on the armrest next to me.

"What are you raising money for?" asked Mum.

"Oh... Aadam." I quickly chewed down the cookie and swallowed. "His application to be a refugee was rejected 'cause he doesn't have any paperwork and they said he's an adult and not sixteen. So he's got to tell the government he's appealing before this Friday but it's gonna cost loads to pay the lawyer to do it."

"How much does he need?" Mum dunked a chocolate digestive in her tea and took a bite.

"About four thousand pounds."

"FOUR THOUSAND POUNDS!" she spluttered. "How will you raise that much in a week?"

"Well, he doesn't need all of it by Friday ... He just

needs a deposit so the lawyer will send off the appeal application. But yeah, he'll need the rest for the other paperwork soon after, I suppose."

"I'll ask some friends for donations. Give me a poster too?" She took another sip of tea.

The front door slammed shut. We both sat up. I peered out of the bay window but didn't see anything. It was probably Samira.

"Yeah, all right. We're making them tomorrow. Thanks, Mum."

"You doing better today?"

I looked at her as if to say, "Can we not go there," and thankfully Samira burst into the room.

"Hey! What's for dinner? Have you already eaten?" She slung her tartan rucksack off her shoulder and dropped it onto the floor, then took her cardigan off, her long brown hair hanging loose down her back. "I'm starving."

"As-salaamu Alaikum, beta." Mum pushed herself off the sofa and went to the door. "I'll warm it up. We were waiting for you to come home. Ahmed should be getting dropped off from swimming club soon too."

Samira followed Mum out of the room and ran upstairs. I picked up the remote and switched the TV on, thankful she'd saved me from talking to Mum about Dad again.

≣

At lunch the next day, we met up in the library to make the posters for the penalty shoot-out. I was on PowerPoint moving text around, while Sami and Mark were telling me what looked best.

"Make 'VIP' red," said Sami. "It has to be the word that everyone sees first."

"Everyone's gonna see *David* in his kit first." I highlighted "VIP" and changed the color anyway.

"We should put these out in other schools too, you know," said Mark, looking at his phone. "Grace said she would."

"Yeah, she did," said Sami, pulling his chair in closer to me.

"Yeah, but then we'd have too many people. Would David even be able to defend that many goals?" I glanced at a Year Seven who'd pulled out the chair at the computer next to me. I nodded at him as he sat down, staring at my screen. Man, I loved the googly-eyed look this poster was giving him.

"He's saved more goals than any other goalie in the Premiership this season! He sure can!" said Mark, his arms hanging over his knees as he watched me enlarge the photo of David.

"Do you think we should add the team logo?" asked Sami.

"Yeahh! That would make it even more professional!" I switched tabs and started googling.

"Yeah but then people will think the shoot-out is to do with the club, so maybe we shouldn't," said Mark.

"Yeah, good point," I said, switching back to the poster.

"This is the computer area." Mrs. Akhtar, our librarian, was showing a new girl around. We all turned to looked at them and then back to our screen, waiting until they left. Her voice grew more distant as they walked away. "You can use the computers at break time, lunchtime, and after school. It does get busy as you can see, so sometimes you have to wait till you can use one. I'll just show you where the printer is . . ."

"Hey! Do you think we can increase the price of tickets now we've got David? Maybe five pounds a ticket?" asked Mark.

"Five pounds a kick?" asked Sami.

"Yeah. I mean he's Premiership. Why wouldn't you pay that?"

"Nah, 'course I would. But I could probably only buy one kick." Sami leaned forward.

"If we sell one hundred tickets, that means we'll have five hundred pounds," I said.

"I reckon we'll sell loads more than that. Everyone will want to score against David," said Mark. "Even if half of each year group buy a ticket, that's still five times ninety. What's that?"

I did the maths in my head. Working together like this gave me a buzz. It was like I didn't have any problems or anything else to worry about.

"Four hundred and fifty," shouted Sami. "Oh my God, that's two thousand two hundred and fifty pounds with every year group in the school! Over half of Aadam's target. Okay, let's put five pounds on the poster!"

I added "£5 per kick," then looked at Sami and Mark. "I think it'll be well worth it!"

"Yeah, it will," said Sami.

"Make the date bigger and put it in bold," said Mark.

"Or even in yellow," added Sami. "It'll stand out more."

"Yeah, but can everyone read yellow font? Don't it make your eyes go funny?" I said, highlighting the text and making it yellow.

"Yeah, that doesn't work. If we do that, the background has to be black."

"See, told you!" I elbowed Sami.

"Are you Ali?" said someone behind me. "Can I talk to you?"

I turned to see who it was.

It was Mustafa.

He just had to turn up and ruin everything.

Chapter 16

I shifted in my chair and looked at Sami and Mark in a panic, unfolding my fists. I had clenched them without even realizing.

Sami sat up and looked at me and then at Mustafa. "Uhhh . . . I gotta go to the toilet."

My face must've looked as hot as it felt.

Sami turned to Mark, and all of a sudden Mark also got up. "I'll be back in ten," he said as he stood, putting his chair back at the table it belonged to.

Mustafa grabbed Sami's chair and sat next to me. Man, he was confident.

"Do you know who I am?" he said, leaning forward with his arms on his knees.

I continued staring at the screen. I didn't know

what to say. If I said yes, he'd know I'd been ignoring him. If I said no, he might be able to tell I was lying.

I could feel him staring at me. "I mean, I knew Dad had other kids," he said. "I knew you were somewhere in Manchester. But I thought you were much older and I definitely had no idea we were at the same school. Dad blurted it out by mistake last night."

Mistake?

Dad thinks I'm a mistake?

I felt my skin tighten. As if something was crawling up it. My head pounded and felt like it was about to explode.

I thumped the table and screamed in his face. "You know what? I *do* know who you are, but I don't want to know you! Just leave me alone!"

Everyone in the library turned to look at us. Mrs. Akhtar got up from behind her desk.

Mustafa stared at me, his eyes wide. As if I'd shot him in the heart when he'd expected a cookie or something. I turned back to the screen, and he got up.

"Well, maybe I don't want to know you either," he said. "What makes you think you're so good? You're nothing special. Look at you. No wonder Dad doesn't see you anymore." He scraped his chair back and left.

It felt liked he'd punched me in the gut. My stomach hardened, and my chin trembled. I bit my bottom lip to stop myself from crying.

"Ali, can you please leave and come back when you're calmer?" said Mrs. Akhtar.

I took in a small sharp breath. My dad hadn't told Mustafa about me living in the area, when Dad *knew* we've lived in the same house since he left us. He knew *exactly* where we were. He'd seen me the other day and *still* not told his "chosen" son. And it was because I wasn't good enough. A mistake. He'd said it himself.

I saved the poster and logged out of my account, picked up my rucksack, and got up, the pain in my chest turning into rage once again. How dare he? I tried my best not to stomp my way to the door.

Sami and Mark were waiting outside.

"What did that boy want?" asked Sami.

I ignored him and walked ahead. There was no way I wanted them to know my dad had cheated on my mum and then chosen his new spawn over us.

Sami rushed in front of me and blocked my path. "Remember how you made me tell you what was bothering me when I wanted to go back to Syria? In fact, you chased me all the way to the airport because you knew I was hurting and that I might do something stupid. Now it's my turn to be there for you. Come on, man, tell us what's happened."

I remembered now that I'd told Sami about my dad leaving us when he first got here a few months ago and was upset about leaving Syria. My stomach rolled, thinking about how I was fine to talk about it back then, but now, knowing Dad was living near us and his chosen golden boy went to *my* school wound me up so much I couldn't bear it. Dad didn't even want to mention my name. And when he had, it was by mistake. And that hurt deep in the pit of my stomach.

I walked a little further and pushed the door into the nearest boys' toilets to check if anyone was in there. It was empty, just the soap foam left splatted all over the sinks. The sound of kids running around and chatting filtered in through the open windows. The smell of unflushed urine hung heavy in the air, and I tried not to breathe it in.

Sami and Mark followed me inside, their faces mirroring their confusion.

"Bro, what is it?" said Sami.

"Yeah, come on, Ali." Mark tapped my arm. "I've never seen you like this. I thought we were mates . . ."

I swallowed. It hurt to say it, but I had to. They were my friends.

"That boy was my brother—my half brother. And the man that gave me his number the other day after we met David at the shops . . . he was my dad. Well, *our* dad."

Sami's and Mark's jaws dropped.

Chapter 17

"*So that's why you've* been acting all weird!" Sami said.

I shuffled my feet and plunged my hands deep into my pockets. It felt odd to call him my half brother out loud. The words hit differently.

Mustafa was *half of me*. Mustafa was 50 percent my family. Not really as far removed as I'd like. I felt sick thinking about it.

"Listen." Mark put his hand on my arm. "Nothin's changed just 'cause your brother's coming to this school. We'll ignore him and pretend he doesn't exist. I mean, he didn't until now, anyway." He pulled his hand away, looking pleased with himself.

They just didn't get it. How could I ignore him? I'd tried and it hadn't worked. Every time I saw Mustafa, I remembered how little we meant to my dad—he'd gone and forgotten about us. And now Mustafa had confirmed that was true with his words. Dad had chosen his new family because we just weren't worthy of his attention, or love, or even time.

"Let's go back in and finish them posters and get them printed. That boy that doesn't exist has gone anyway." Mark grinned. "Then I'll treat you to some slimy, gooey pizza. That'll cheer you up! It's nearly time for the Year Eights' lunch anyway. Let's be first in the queue for once." Mark bumped my shoulder with his as he headed back to the library.

I forced myself to smile at Sami, who glanced at me as he pulled the door open. But my whole chest hurt.

"Sorry, Miss," I muttered as I passed the librarian's desk and headed to the computer. Sami and Mark were already in their chairs waiting for me.

After we'd finalized all the details on the charity shoot-out poster, I pressed print. Sami scuffed his chair back and ran to the printer. He rushed to us, beaming.

"Look, man!" He held the color posters up over his face.

"Look at David!" said Mark.

"We're gonna make that four-thousand-pound

target, aren't we?" I said. "Come on, let's go and stick them *everywhere* before next lesson. Give me one." I put my hand out, and Sami slipped me a sheet.

"Miss? Can we put one up in here?" I asked, walking up to Mrs. Akhtar.

"Yes, of course. Here." She handed me a ball of Blu Tack. "You can put it anywhere on that wall." She pointed to a noticeboard full of announcements.

"Thanks, Miss."

Sticking the posters up around school made me feel like I had a purpose. I straightened my shoulders as I walked. Maybe I wasn't the loser Dad and Mustafa thought I was. Should I be defined by my dad and his ridiculous choices? Nope. I couldn't let Mustafa's words take over my brain. I had to focus on the fundraiser for Aadam's fees and try to forget about my non-existent dad and his "chosen son." I mean, I'd got to thirteen without letting him get to me, so I would just have to block him out again.

Chapter 18

After school, we'd agreed to meet Mark in the science block.

"All right?" I said when I spotted him at the foot of the stairs near the biology labs, leaning over the banister, spying on someone.

Mark turned and waved us over, putting his finger on his lips.

Sami rushed down to join him, and I followed, staying quiet. I tiptoed past Mark, peeking around the corner, into the corridor in the main building.

Nathan was pointing at our poster and talking to a small group of Year Eights who were reading it. "It's not true, there is *no way* David Mora would be working with a bunch of schoolkids, and definitely not them three. Don't waste your money. I reckon it's a scam."

I jumped off the last step and turned in to the corridor, Sami just behind me.

The kids walked off and Nathan spun, looking smug. His face dropped when he saw us. Then he straightened his shoulders. "Your scam to raise money for ISIS in Syria is gonna be exposed!" he shouted before grabbing his rucksack off the floor and stomping off.

I didn't know what to say. I looked at Mark and Sami.

Mark laughed. "How did he come up with that?"

Me and Sami burst out laughing too.

"Actually this *is* his racist brain, so maybe it wasn't that hard for him!" Sami roared.

"What a leap, man!" I said.

"Come on, let's get to the park." Mark wiped his eyes with his sleeves.

The only way to deal with Nathan's ridiculousness was to laugh at it.

Sami put the ball down, making it ready to be booted towards our makeshift goal for our penalty practice, then started doing walking lunges to warm up.

Mark would be in goal like always, and me, Sami, and Elijah were going to take turns to shoot.

"Oh, yeah!" said Mark, taking a swig of water. "I forgot to tell you guys with all the poster and Nathan stuff ... I spoke to David this morning. He threw my ball over the hedge and I shouted thanks and then he asked how we were getting on."

"Check you out! Best mates with David Mora!" I said.

Mark grinned, looking well pleased with himself. "He said his gardener's been putting my footballs aside for me."

"You should ask him to come practice with us before the fundraiser!" said Elijah, jogging on the spot. "I can't believe you guys actually met him."

"Yeah! Be cheeky and ask," I said, trying to balance on one leg as I pulled my foot up to my butt to stretch my quads. I put my arm out to stop wobbling. "Apart from it being epic to be seen with him, it would also be the best way of us getting more people wanting to take part!"

Sami stood up from his lunge. "If he came, Nathan would be sooo jealous!"

The pleasure of that possibility was obvious on Sami's face.

"Ask him, yeah?" I nodded at Mark.

"Well, he actually said he might drop in at school with his management to check out the grounds and layout and stuff," said Mark, as if it was just some random person and this wasn't a big deal.

"No way!" I grinned, jogging on the spot.

Mark nodded. "He said he'll come unannounced when he's in the area so there's no fuss or cameras. No one will know—well, apart from Mrs. Greenwood and maybe Mrs. Hack, obviously."

"Yesss!" said Elijah, pulling on his tracksuit top over his T-shirt. "Nathan is going to melt into a puddle when he sees us with him!"

Sami laughed as he rolled the ball under his foot. "He is going to die, especially 'cause he thinks we're raising money for ISIS and lying about David!"

"Nah!" said Elijah. "Man, that guy's mind is messed up."

I laughed. It felt good to be out in the late-afternoon sun with my boys—a place I definitely felt wanted and good enough.

"But yeah, if I see him again I'll ask if he'll do a practice session," Mark shouted as he ran off into goal.

Sami took five steps back from the ball and stared at Mark, who was now in place.

"Sami!" I said, and he turned. I jogged up to him and whispered in his ear, "Stare at both the goalposts, to confuse him before you take the kick."

Sami nodded and I stepped back.

Elijah blew the whistle, and Sami angled his body left and then right, then ran up to the ball, kicking it hard and low to Mark's left. Mark leaped in the opposite direction.

"GOOOOAAAALL!" we all screamed.

"Ha! You confused him!" I went up and fist-bumped Sami.

"Beginner's luck and all that!" shouted Mark.

"Here." Elijah passed me the whistle. It was his turn.

Mark kicked the ball back out to us, and Elijah stopped it with his boot, then dribbled into position. He closed his eyes and took a deep breath, then ran, kicking the ball higher this time, and to the right. Mark reached out, but his hand just missed and Elijah scored.

"GOOOOAAAALL!" we all screamed. Again!

"That was a fluke!" said Mark.

"Yeah, yeah!" I said. "Watch out, David Mora, we're comin' for ya!"

After practice, I carefully pulled the pristine posters for the fundraiser from my physics textbook and handed them out to everyone. "There's three each. Put them up on your way home. Ask in busy shops near bus stops or something. We've only got, like, two and a half weeks and we need a massive crowd."

"To get enough money for Aadam's fees," added Sami.

"I'll get one up in my mum's pharmacy," Elijah said, taking his copies. "Five pounds?" He stared at the poster.

"It's for a kick against David, but is that too much?" I asked, handing out the small balls of Blu Tack I'd managed to get from Mrs. Akhtar in the library.

"I mean, he is a Premier League footballer, so it is well worth it, but I'll only be able to stretch to one ticket."

Sami zipped up his rucksack and put his arm through a strap. "Yeah, me too. But it's okay, we'll have to limit it to one ticket per person anyway, otherwise the rich kids would be the only ones with all the kicks."

Elijah nodded. "You should make the tickets look like Willy Wonka's."

"What, like gold?" I asked.

"Yeah, proper special."

"Good idea! Sami, you think we can get gold paper from anywhere at school?" I asked.

"I'll get it," said Mark.

"Ohh, yeah! I forgot you were megarich now."

"Shame I can't ask my mum to just pay for Aadam's legal fees though." Mark kicked up some grass.

Sami nudged Mark. "Aadam would never let you pay for it all. He knows you care and that's enough for him. Anyway . . . if your mum did pay, we'd never get to score against Mora!"

Mark fist-bumped Sami. "Ha ha! Yep!"

Chapter 19

"*Hello, boys.*" Mrs. Webster, my old Year Seven PE teacher, strolled over to Sami, Mark, and me in the lunch hall queue the next day, wearing the school tracksuit top and shorts.

"Errr . . . hello, Miss," we all said together.

"Mrs. Hack and Mrs. Greenwood have spoken to me about this fundraiser and I'm going to help you set it up." She raised her neatly drawn-on brows and smiled. "Do you think you could meet me after lunch to go through the details?"

"Yes!" said Sami, like an eager puppy.

"Miss, when can we start selling the tickets?" I asked, picking up a tray.

"That's what I also want to talk about. I'll help

you sell them and take care of all the cash. Sami, I've spoken to your dad about handing it over to him once we've collected it all, so we don't have a bunch of thirteen-year-olds running around school with loads of money!"

Sami's mouth dropped. "He didn't tell me he'd already spoken to you."

Mrs. Webster smiled. "Ah, see, we're all on top of things over here! Mrs. Greenwood has also spoken to Mr. Mora's agent and gone over the details. You got a bit of a catch there, didn't you?" Her eyes sparkled, and I realized this was as exciting for the teachers as it was for us.

She nodded at Sami and pointed behind him. The lunch queue had moved on ahead of us, and there was a massive gap. We all pushed our trays along the counter to where the staff stood.

"I'll have a tuna melt panini to go, thanks," Mrs. Webster said to a dinner lady, then looked at us. "Do you have the tickets ready?"

"Yeah, we printed them at break," said Mark. "We just need to cut them all 'cause we printed four per page." Mark's mum had dropped off some gold paper just before break for his "emergency art project he'd forgotten about," but the printing hadn't worked out as well as we'd thought.

"Okay, I'll ask the form tutors to put a notice out about the tickets in form time tomorrow. And we could sell them in the playground after school next Tuesday so everyone isn't holding on to them for too long and risk them getting lost or crushed in their bags. What do you think? That gives everyone the weekend to ask their parents or guardians for the money and whatnot."

"That sounds awesome, Miss!" said Sami.

"Okay, great. I'll let you get your lunch. Pop into the sports office after you're done and we'll discuss timing and everything in more detail, okay?" She reached over the counter, and the dinner lady handed her a paper bag, which, judging by the fishy smell, must've been her tuna panini, and she strolled off.

A buzz of excitement went right through me as I moved my tray towards the cashier. We were so close to doing something amazing. We were on fire. I wasn't going to let anything get in my head now. Not Mustafa. Not my so-called dad.

Sami and Aadam came round in the evening, and we all sat around the kitchen table cutting the tickets into neat rectangles. Elijah's idea of printing gold tickets hadn't worked out, because the ink didn't set on the paper properly and got smudgy. So we'd stuck to good old yellow school paper. Sami felt bad that Mark's mum had come to school especially to drop it off for his "special project," but I didn't—he shouldn't have had to lie about it in the first place.

"Ahmed, you need to get closer to the border so it's a proper rectangle. Can you do that one again?" Sami said to my brother. We'd included him since he was moping around anyway, and we could do with the help.

"Have you spoken to your lawyer again?" I asked Aadam as I tried to get as close to the black border as I could. "Is he sending off the appeal form?"

Aadam sighed. "Yeah. Sami's dad and my friends at unaccompanied minor center helped pay the deposit, so I had my meeting with my lawyer, but I need to get the paperwork in on time."

"Dad says he's pretty sure Aadam will get 'leave to remain' in the next application because this time it will be done properly and we'll have proof he's a kid and not an adult," said Sami, setting his scissors down and having a drink of apple juice.

"Oh, that's good," I said.

"What sort of paperwork do you need?" asked Ahmed. A good question; I'd let him have it.

"I need to show them proof I am sixteen. So my mum is trying to get my old head teacher to help. I lost all my official certificates in Lebanon—I think the men who forced me to work for them threw everything away, because the certificates were in my bag one day and then they weren't there the next." Aadam picked his scissors up again.

"How come you were in Lebanon?" I asked. "I thought you lived in Syria."

"I did. I went to Lebanon first after leaving Syria, but I was attacked by a bunch of men and they forced me to work for them and beat me up. They treat Syrians so badly because millions of us ended up there and the Lebanese ran out of money, and so they blame us. That's why I escaped and went to Turkey." Aadam smiled at Sami. "That's where I met Sami and his family."

"Oh, right." I didn't know what to say. He'd been through so much. Man, I hoped we'd make the four-thousand-pounds target so he could get his refugee status and just live life without having to worry about this sort of stuff again.

Sami picked up a new sheet to cut. "The lawyer thinks he's got a good chance of winning the fresh claim because he can use the photos my dad has of Syria to prove Aadam can't go back there since it's not safe. And Aadam's mum has sent photos of what happened to his house and the conditions she's living in."

"I lost all of that with my phone, so my first application was not very strong," said Aadam, concentrating on snipping around a corner. Then he chuckled. "It's funny, they say to me, 'You came illegally.' But to claim asylum I had to come here illegally because there was no way for me to apply from Syria!"

"It's a stupid system. Makes no sense." Sami put his scissors down and looked at me. "Plus the Home Office said Aadam was twenty-five! Did I tell you that?"

"No way!" I said. "They actually said you were twenty-five?!"

"Yeah." Aadam took a sip of juice. "They said one of my friends from Afghanistan was thirty!"

"Yup. They just made Aadam's age up!" said Sami. "That's why he was on the streets and no one would help him when we found each other again that night when we went to get a burger. Remember?" He looked at me.

"I forgot about that!" Aadam smiled at me. "Akhi, you were there with Sami and me from the start!" He nudged my elbow. "I knew you were a top guy as soon as you said salaam to me even though I was unwashed and in filthy clothes. You treated me like a human, when most people just avoided me."

I smiled back, thinking of that night me and Sami had gone to get a chicken burger and Sami had spotted Aadam in the queue. Sami thought he'd never see him again after they'd been separated in Turkey. He didn't even know if Aadam had made the boat journey. I'd left them to it, but it looked emotional.

"And then we'd all ended up in a homeless shelter with Mum, Dad, and Sara." Sami sighed. "Man, I'm glad those days are over." He shook his head and picked his scissors up again.

Ahmed squirmed in his seat. I suppose it was a lot for him to hear. I think this was the first time any of us had talked about Sami's and Aadam's journeys like this. It kind of showed how we'd become such good friends.

"Are we going to help your mum too?" Ahmed asked Aadam.

Aadam looked down as if he was blinking away

tears. "I have been working to send her money, but now this legal-fees situation has come up, she won't let me send any more. I have begged her to leave Syria and come here, but she won't leave our house. Even though it is now a shell. She says we will have nothing to our family name if she leaves."

"Can we do anything to help?" I asked.

"My dad has organized an operation for her leg," said Sami. "Once that's done we're gonna try again to see if we can persuade her to leave."

I couldn't imagine how hard that must be for Aadam to deal with on top of everything else.

"If it wasn't for Sami and his family, I wouldn't have anybody here." Aadam smiled gently at Sami and had a faraway look in his eyes.

"Do you want to go back when it's safe?" asked Ahmed, snipping off the extra paper around his already-cut ticket.

"More than anything in the world," said Aadam. He dropped his scissors on the table.

"What do you miss the most?" Wow, Ahmed was interviewing my boy hard.

Aadam smiled. "Oh, I miss hearing Fairouz first thing in the morning... She's a famous Arab singer that so many Syrians wake up to. I miss my mum's food and booza—that's a stretchy, chewy Syrian ice cream. So much!" His blue eyes sparkled, then his smile dropped. "It's a year since I left and I thought the war would've been over by now and we'd all have gone back, but . . . it doesn't look like it's going to stop anytime soon." He shrugged. "It's hard because we didn't just lose family and friends, or our homes, we lost our whole lives . . . who we were."

Sami nodded hard as he cut around a ticket.

"Must be hard to start again from scratch," I said.

"I hope no one else ever has to do this after us." Aadam picked up his scissors again and started cutting. I guess he was done talking.

My phone buzzed. "Mark's video-calling," I said, showing the boys my screen. "Oi oi, Mark!" I said.

It looked like he was out walking. "What you lot doing?" he said.

"Cutting out the tickets. Where are you?" I asked.

"In my garden. Where else? I'm bored. Got nothin' to do."

"What about Grace?" Sami asked.

"What about her? She's busy, just like you lot are. Everyone's got a life but me."

"Just come round, man!" I said, showing him Sami, Aadam, Ahmed, and the pile of cut tickets. "Could do with your help."

"I wish I could," Mark said, stopping in front of a humongous tree trunk. "But Callum and Mum are home all evening and apparently we're going out for a 'special meal' later." It was obvious from his face he wasn't happy about it. "Stupid Callum. Thinks he's my dad."

"I'm sorry, mate," I said. It was weird what we were both going through. There was Mark, struggling because this crudhead wanted to be his dad. And then there was me, struggling because my real dad had turned up and still didn't want to be my dad.

"Right, I can't wait until I see you guys so I'm just gonna tell you now—I've got some *amazing* news!" Mark suddenly sounded chirpy. A bit too chirpy. Maybe he'd noticed my face had changed. I sat up, trying to look brighter and happier too. "So, I got one of my balls back over the hedge earlier and David said we could have a prize for the best penalty scored!"

"Seriously? Like, he'll judge them?"

"Yeah, and he said he'll do a behind-the-scenes stadium tour with the winner, including changing rooms . . . AND we can go too 'cause he wants to keep his promise from the day we stopped his car from being keyed!" Mark grinned.

"Oh boy, behind the scenes and CHANGING ROOMS TOO! I hope *I* win!" I said.

I turned the phone to show Mark Sami's and Aadam's excited faces. If they were dogs they'd have been panting.

"I hope I win!" said Sami.

"Yeah, but you're all going anyway, so you don't even have to try," said Ahmed with the most serious face.

We all burst out laughing.

Chapter 20

It was Thursday afternoon, and we were picking up Ahmed from his school football club. Mum had forced me to go with her. Well, she convinced me that if I helped her carry the ten kilograms of rice at the supermarket, my muscles would grow. And to be honest, I didn't need more convincing. I wanted bigger arms.

It was weird to go back and look out at my old primary school. Everything seemed so small now, when it had felt huge when I was there.

Ahmed pulled the car door open and scrambled into the back.

"What are you doing here?" he said, gawping at me. "Last week you said you were never ever going to come and drop me off or pick me up from football ever again." He tutted, and clicked his seat belt into place.

I turned from the passenger seat and looked at him. "That was 'cause you took five hundred hours getting changed and then expected me to carry your kit bag like I was your manservant."

Mum turned the car engine on and glanced at both of us. "Oh, don't start fighting, you two. Ahmed, I asked Ali to come because I want him to help me with the rice. And you should've thanked him for stepping in last week for me and picking you up when no one else could."

I smirked at Ahmed, and he rolled his eyes and folded his arms before looking out the window.

We entered the supermarket car park, and Mum drove into a spot and pulled up her handbrake. The sky was overcast with clouds, but it was bright, as if the sun was going to burst through at any moment. Just as we all unclicked our seat belts, a car reversed into the spot in front of ours. It was a beat-up maroon car that looked an awful lot like . . . I shrank into my seat. It was Dad . . . with Mustafa.

They'd come to the supermarket at the same time as us.

Mum glanced up as she grabbed her handbag from my footwell, did a double take, and looked away again quickly. She clearly didn't want to make eye contact.

"Just hold on, Ahmed." She put her arm on his knee through the gap in the front seats to stop him from getting out. "Stay in the car."

I wasn't sure if Ahmed had clicked why.

Dad slammed his car door shut. He had his back to us, and I hoped he wouldn't go into the back to get a bag out or anything. He followed Mustafa, who had already made his way past a few rows of cars.

I put my head back on my seat and clenched my jaw, watching them both swan off to do their special shopping together. Dad and son.

"Okay, boys, we need to talk," said Mum, turning to face us both. She looked at me and nodded towards Ahmed as if to say to me, "This talk is for him." She then turned to Ahmed. "I know it's been a while since you saw your dad anywhere. But that might change, as he has moved back into the area."

"Has he?!" Ahmed sounded excited.

"Yes, Ahmed. I think it was just over a week ago. So you might see him." She looked at me. "Because obviously we're going to be shopping in the same places and be in the same neighborhood—you're going to bump into him. And so, I want you to promise me that if you do see him, just talk to him with respect. Remember, he's your dad."

"No, he's not. You did everything all by yourself," I said.

"Ali, yes, he is. He's your dad ... And he made a choice. But that does not mean that you will show up our family or show up the way that I raised you by being disrespectful to him. Do you understand?"

I looked down at my lap, tempted to pull my phone out to show Mum I wasn't interested in this conversation.

"I want to see him. What does he look like now? Do you think he'll want to see us?" said Ahmed, and I swallowed back the feeling of despair rising inside me. My poor baby brother. How could Dad have just forgotten about him?

"You know what he looks like, Ahmed. You've seen his photos and he was at that wedding a few years ago."

"I don't remember." His voice broke.

If I could've cried right then, I would have. I gulped back the forming tears and pulled out my phone. I couldn't deal with this. I had to focus on something else.

Mum stroked my cheek before reaching for Ahmed. "Oh, my baby, come here." She tried to hug Ahmed through the gap between our front seats.

"Look, he might want to meet up now he's closer. He did see Samira. He might be taking it slowly. Let's just give it some time, okay?"

Huh? He met up with Samira? And she didn't tell us . . . or take us?

My nostrils flared. Maybe he just didn't need us boys. Samira and Mustafa were enough.

"Okay, let's go and get that shop," she said. I could feel her watching me as I scrolled through my playlist. She took a deep breath and pushed her door open.

Ahmed jumped out and slammed his door shut.

"Come on!" Mum ducked her head in.

"I don't want to go," I said.

"Ali, I need help with the rice because of my back. You know that. Come on."

"No. I don't want to go in there. You can get a supermarket assistant to help you put the rice in the trolley. And then when you get to the car, I'll put it in for you, and I'll take it into the house. You don't need me in the supermarket."

Mum sighed and dropped her hands by her side.

"Okay, no problem. Stay here on your phone or whatever. Just don't walk off anywhere. I won't be long; I'm just getting rice and a couple of other things. I don't want to have to look for you once I get back to the car."

"I won't move." I shrugged, shrinking into my seat.

Mum shut her door and walked off with Ahmed, avoiding passing by Dad's car.

I sat facing his old banger. Right in front of me.

I wasn't sure if this was a good idea. If he came back before Mum, he might see me. But if he was doing a big shop, we might be gone before he'd even paid.

I decided I'd keep looking up to check. I glanced at my window—it was open enough for me to hear them coming. And if I did, I'd duck.

Chapter 21

I heard some voices heading towards the car and slid right down my seat, into the footwell. The voices got closer, and my heart started racing.

What if Dad recognized Mum's car and was coming to check it out? He was going to catch me hiding here. How would that look?!

The voices were now next to the car, and it sounded like two people. The car boot clicked and whooshed up, and I breathed out. It was Mum and Ahmed.

I sat back in my seat before they found me scrunched up like a hibernating hedgehog.

Mum pulled her door open and chucked her bag in between our seats. "Can't believe they ran out of rice!" She slid into her seat and pulled her door closed. "This is what happens when Aldi has a sale. Us Asians love a bargain!"

"It's your lucky day," Ahmed said to me, handing me a Kit Kat and unwrapping his Kinder egg. "You don't have to carry any heavy bags."

I wasn't in the mood to eat, so I put the chocolate in the glove box and watched Mum fumble around with her key while keeping her eyes fixed ahead of her. It looked like she was rushing to get it into the ignition. "I take it you didn't see—"

"No," Mum replied before I could finish.

I suddenly felt lighter. "Can we leave quickly, please?"

"That's the plan!" Mum reversed out of the parking spot and drove fast towards the exit. I looked down at my phone to make sure I didn't spot Dad or Mustafa by accident.

"I'll have to try and get to the Asian stores in Levenshulme sometime this week." Mum tutted, then signaled left and turned in to a side street. I put my phone into my pocket, as the battery was low, and looked out at the houses whooshing by. A few streets down I spotted men getting out of parked cars in their white robes and topis. I glanced at the clock on the car dashboard. They must've been going early for Asar prayers. I leaned against my window to get a glimpse of the mosque.

A boy around Ahmed's age ran up to someone who looked like his dad, and the man put his arm around him. My shoulders locked, and my hands fisted. *I can't even go to the mosque, because I don't have a dad or adult to take me.* The last time I went on a regular day was for Jum'ah when Uncle Azeem had visited from America and taken me with him.

My throat tightened as I pictured Dad and Mustafa laughing and joking as they went to pray. I bet Mustafa could go whenever he wanted with Dad. Not me though—*I* had to rely on Mum's friends' husbands to offer to take me, or else we'd only go on Eid when they opened up the mosque to women too.

By the time we pulled up outside our house, it felt like every vein in my head was throbbing and my head was going to explode.

Bursting into the front room, I found Samira sprawled across the floor with all her uni notes. She must've cut her hair, because it was up in a short, spiky ponytail and looked like she had a pineapple on the top of her head.

I grabbed the remote control from the armrest of the sofa and sat down on the middle cushion of the three-seater. Mum slammed the front door shut, and Ahmed raced up the stairs. I went to the music channels and stopped on MTV, where they were playing Drake.

"Turn it down. I've got an exam tomorrow!" Samira glared at me, then went back to her notes.

I pressed the plus button on the remote and turned the volume up.

Samira got on her knees and reached for the remote.

I pulled my arm back, and she tried to grab it.

"Why are you SO annoying!" she shouted, still reaching for the remote.

"Why are you?" I shouted. "You're the one who met Dad! You traitor!" I put my head back on the sofa and closed my eyes. I wasn't supposed to come out with that right now. I was supposed to keep the peace in this family. Why couldn't I have just waited till I was calmer, man?

"Who told you?"

I opened my eyes. Samira was still on the floor, now with her back to me.

"Mum."

Samira fiddled with her pen, clicking the push

button repeatedly. "He asked to see me, so I thought I'd give him a chance to explain why he just left." She shrugged.

I switched off the TV. "What did he say?"

"He said that when he got my letter he thought it'd be best for us if he just left us to it."

"What letter?" I put my arms on my knees and leaned forward.

Samira lowered her head and stopped clicking her pen. "I wrote him a letter when he said he was moving in with the woman he'd married and told him that I didn't wanna see him anymore. I was only eleven and just so sick of being passed between Mum and Dad like a tennis ball during their arguments in that first week after he left." She looked at her nails. "I didn't think he'd actually just do what I asked, though. I thought he'd fight for us instead. That's what I was trying to get him to do."

I sighed. I didn't even remember the arguments. I didn't remember anything but Mum crying. Maybe I'd blocked it out. "It's not your fault he did that, you know."

"Well, it kinda is, isn't it? What if I hadn't written it? Would he have still seen us? Would you and Ahmed have had Dad in your life?" Her voice broke.

It hit me that she'd been living with this guilt for years. I got on the floor. "Sam, it's not your fault. You're his kid too, remember?"

"Yeah, I know." Samira sighed. She opened her folder and started lifting her notes of paper into it. "I'm gonna go work upstairs. You listen to your crappy rap." She smiled at me but I could see her eyes brimming.

I forced myself to smile even though I just wanted to hug her and tell her to let it all out. Anger coursed through me.

"I hate that man," I blurted. "He didn't just ruin my life. He ruined all four of our lives."

Samira got up, holding her folder to her chest. "What do you want him to do? What's the point of being so angry? He's useless."

I sat back, leaning on the sofa, and thought about it. What did I want? I wanted to be seen. I just wanted him to *see* me. He didn't even acknowledge I was his actual son, the same as Mustafa.

Samira held the front room door open. "We got this far without him and we will be fine, Ali. Just let it go. It's not good for you."

She was right. I had to let it go. I had to focus on other things. I had to focus on the fundraiser and just move on. Ignore Mustafa. Ignore Dad. Focus on getting Aadam's money for his appeal and on my mates. The people who were actually there for me.

Chapter 22

It was Friday morning, and the whole school had gathered in the hall for assembly. Mrs. Greenwood walked across the stage in her shiny black high heels and stopped in the middle to face us.

"Good morning, everyone," she said.

I sat up to show I was listening.

"So, we've got a very exciting week at the end of this month. And I thought it was time to tell you more about the very special event we've got coming up on Friday, twenty-seventh of May, after school. I'm sure you'll have seen the posters by now." She walked to the right of the stage and then back to the middle. "When Mrs. Hack came to me and asked if we could help a group of Heath Academy students organize a special charity penalty shoot-out, to start with I said I wasn't sure. It's almost the end of the year and we're all busy with GCSE exams and end-of-term assessments. But then I thought about it. We celebrate Refugee Week each year. It's coming up again in a month. We read books about refugees. So why don't we walk the walk as well as talk the talk? And why not walk the walk for someone who is a family member to one of our own students. Someone from our own community. Aadam al-Rashid is a part of our community—"

"No he's not!" someone shouted from the audience.

Mrs. Greenwood paused and looked around, her eyes laser sharp, as if she'd zap the person into a puddle right there if she caught them.

The hall went ultraquiet and people shuffled in their seats, looking around for the culprit.

I spotted Nathan with his hand over his mouth and head bowed, trying not to laugh. Tom sat next to him, giving him evils.

Nathan. 'Course it was him.

I nudged Sami. He glanced at Nathan too and shook his head in disgust.

Mrs. Greenwood continued, "As I was saying, Aadam al-Rashid is a member of our community. As you all know, we have refugees in our school from Syria, but sadly Aadam has been denied that right because he doesn't have the documents needed to prove his age. He's sixteen. The same age as most of our Year Elevens." Mrs. Greenwood looked at the empty seats at the side of the hall where the Year Elevens would usually be sitting if they weren't on exam leave. "Aadam's mum sent him to England because we don't have an ongoing war here and we believe in education. She thought we would give him opportunities to succeed that he might not get in Syria until he's too old to make the most of them." She looked around at all of us. "So let's help him. Let's give him the chance at life he deserves. Let's kick those penalties and raise money to help him stay!" She raised her arms as if she'd won something, and everyone burst into a big round of applause.

Mrs. Greenwood put her hands out, indicating we should stop. She waited for the hall to quiet before continuing. "And of course you will have heard by now that Mr. David Mora has volunteered his extremely special skills for this penalty shoot-out. David Mora wants to help Aadam too. How exciting!" She put her hands together and grinned, and lots of kids shouted, "YESSS!"

She continued. "You will be able to buy tickets next week on Tuesday after school. You'll all have had the letter from Mrs. Webster yesterday. Now, we do need to keep numbers limited because it is on our school fields and we can't have *everybody* here. We're a big school, but not *that* big. And we don't want to tire out Mr. Mora. And so, we have decided to limit the penalty kicks to our students only. And only one ticket per student. BUT we will be selling entry tickets for anybody who wants to come and watch.

"It's going to be an extremely special event. And I'm also very pleased to announce that I've had a chat with Aadam, and he will hopefully be coming in to speak to you in June during Refugee Week. Because it's important to hear about his journey too."

I looked at Sami with my mouth open, and Sami nodded smugly. "She called Dad yesterday," he mouthed.

"And with any luck, we will raise the amount Aadam needs to appeal for his asylum case and it will be successful. We hope he will be given refugee status and be allowed to stay with his family here in Stockport. Sami's family." She scanned the Year Eight rows and smiled when she spotted Sami.

Everybody turned to look at him too. Nathan's eyes narrowed into slits. I looked away, shaking off the evil emitting from him. He was so exhausting.

"Right, let's get you all back to your form rooms. We've got a busy day ahead!"

The Year Tens were already getting up from their chairs before Mrs. Greenwood ushered us out. I spotted Mustafa in the Year Seven row, glaring at me. As soon as we locked eyes, he sneered and looked down.

The crudhead was so up himself.

Chapter 23

After school on Tuesday, me, Sami, and Mark sat down behind a table on the playground with Mrs. Webster watching over us. The penalty shoot-out was next Friday, and after two weeks of planning we were *finally* collecting ticket money.

The sun was beating down, and life was good. And doing something to help Aadam felt amazing. The best thing was, we couldn't sell the tickets fast enough. Kids were dropping a fiver into our empty Celebrations chocolates tub, one after another, and the queue for tickets went right around the sports block. They were selling so fast, I didn't even have time to count how many we had left. All I knew was that the wad of tickets was now getting thin.

A group of Year Eights turned up with the sourest faces I'd seen. "You've not really got David Mora, have you? You're scamming us, right?"

"Nope, we're totally telling the truth," Sami said, smiling. "Otherwise, why would the school let us do this?"

"Well, Nathan said you made it all up for attention."

"Ugh. He would say that." I rolled my eyes.

"It's fine. You don't have to buy any tickets, do you?" said Mark, waving them away. "Next, please!"

They gave us all a look before moving on. Ah well. It was their loss.

A Year Seven kid tried to hand me a fiver, and I nodded at Sami, who took it. He must've been the last of the Year Sevens. They'd all come running out of school and had lined up first before anyone else had probably even packed their bags. I'd noticed Mustafa was nowhere to be seen—the tight git. Not that I expected him to support anything I was a part of. Everyone in school knew who was organizing the shoot-out, and he'd even seen us making the posters. Just as well, really. I didn't want to see him at it. I handed the kid a ticket and read out the number to Mark. "We need your full name. It's for the list."

The kid looked at me, lingered, and grinned, staring right at me.

Weirdo.

"You're Mustafa's brother. Ali, innit?"

What?

A heavy feeling settled in my stomach. My nostrils flared; my head felt hot. How dare he tell people before checking with me! He had no right. He'd already taken everything from me and now, he'd even taken my right to decide if I wanted to tell anyone I had another brother!

I threw the bunch of tickets onto the table and jumped up, toppling my chair.

"Where you going?" Sami called after me, but I wasn't looking back. Only forward.

I marched across the netball court and onto the field, crossing the football pitch, where the Year Sevens had started football practice. All I saw was the sea of red T-shirts. I ran like a bull into the match, straight towards Mustafa, who was dribbling the ball—unaware he was about to be tackled. Hard. My foot struck the ball, and his leg interlocked with mine, and he fell, taking me down with him.

I wrapped my arms around him to get on top of

him and show him who was stronger. I didn't need a dad, and I didn't need a stupid half brother. He wasn't better than me. I *was* good enough.

Mustafa's eyes were wide in panic, but he fought back, wrestling and rolling with me, trying to gain control and get on top.

Someone blew a whistle in the distance.

The next thing I knew, two big hands wedged themselves between our shoulders and pulled us apart.

Oh man. A teacher. Now I was in trouble.

I blinked hard and looked up to say sorry, out of breath.

It was my PE teacher, Mr. Clarke, and ... David Mora.

Oh man. Even worse.

Chapter 24

I wished I was in a hole. Anywhere but here.

"Get up!" said Mr. Clarke to both of us.

Mustafa bounced onto his feet first, dusting off his kit.

David put his hand out to me and helped me up. Maybe he could see the shame oozing out of me.

Mr. Clarke looked all googly-eyed at David. "Um . . . sorry about that. The kids aren't usually rolling around the ground fighting!" He laughed. No one else did. It wasn't funny.

"No worries."

"Are either of you hurt? Mustafa? Ali?" Mr. Clarke glanced at Mustafa, then me.

"No," we both chimed together miserably.

"Come on, back to what you were doing." Mr.

Clarke ushered Mustafa to follow him. "We're in the middle of a game. Just know I'll talk to you both later about this," he said, giving me and Mustafa a "look."

"I'm just gonna have a word, if that's okay?" David put his hand on my shoulder.

I gulped. What if David didn't want to do the fundraiser for Aadam now? I knew I'd mess this up somehow. I shouldn't have got involved.

"Sure, I'll just get back to our game." Mr. Clarke gestured to all the Year Seven boys who had gathered to go back to their pitch.

"What was all that about? Why are you so angry?" asked David, putting his hands in his shorts pockets.

I looked down and swallowed, closing my eyes for a moment to think about what I should say. What was happening to me? Why was I lashing out like this?

The whistle blew. They were playing again.

I looked up and pointed at the match. "He's been telling everyone he's my brother!"

"Okay . . . ?" David tilted his head.

I couldn't take this anymore. "He's *not* my brother! He's my half brother! I didn't even know him until two weeks ago! He can't just come here and tell everyone without checking with me. I was here first!"

"Oh. You just found out about him?" David nudged my shoulder with his arm and we started walking back towards the school.

"Yeah, kind of . . ." I bit my lip and tried to match his long stride.

David waved at a man dressed in a smart business suit at the edge of the field and then put up three fingers as if to say he'd be three minutes, before turning back to me. "That happened to me too. You're not on your own, you know . . ."

It happened to him? I looked up at David and his neatly parted brown hair. Man, he was tall.

"My dad left and went and had another family and next thing I know, when I start playing professionally my little brother, Joe, turns up at my house asking for help. I was livid at first but then when I calmed down, I realized it wasn't his fault." He put his hands back in his pockets.

His dad left him too? But his life seemed so perfect.

"What, because it was your dad's fault?" I asked, still trying to keep up.

"Yeah—my half brother didn't tell my dad to leave us . . . or forget about us, did he?"

"Yeah, true." I guessed he was right. But the ache in

my chest was still there. Even if what David said made sense in my head, deep down it still felt like Mustafa had taken my dad away from me. He was enough and I wasn't.

David patted me on the back. "Right, I better go. My management"—he pointed at the man in the suit—"just wanted to check out the grounds and chat to school security. I'll see you in a few days." He smiled. "And, maybe you should do something about your fight?" He nodded back to the Year Seven match.

I clocked Mustafa rubbing his arm. I swallowed. I had to say sorry even if I didn't want to, otherwise David would think I was a right idiot. I glanced at David. "Okay, I will. Thanks, David. Sorry you had to see that."

"Hey. I get it." He nodded and walked off.

I jogged up to Mustafa, who was now sitting on the bench, and turned to check where David was. He had his arms folded and was chatting to his management person. He kept glancing in our direction.

I put my fist out to bump Mustafa's and opened my lips and closed them again. My mouth just couldn't say "I'm sorry."

Mustafa flinched, then sat up and stiffened. He

pressed his lips together and slowly raised his fist to mine, then pulled it back. "You know, I always thought it would be cool to have an older brother until I actually met you."

I stepped back and stared at him, unsure what to say. Was he dissing me or telling me he felt let down? It felt like both.

"I shouldn't have come at you," I finally said. "That was my bad and I'm sorry." I didn't give him a chance to say anything more, even though I meant it, and left.

I should've gone to help Sami and Mark with the never-ending ticket queue but my muscles felt too tight, as if I wouldn't make the walk. I slowly headed towards the playground, feeling as if Mustafa had punched the air out of me. I sat down on a bench and put my head in my hands. My skull pulsed with the worst headache I'd ever had. I could've handled this differently. I wasn't the only one hurting or feeling let down by Dad's decisions—Mustafa was too.

"You okay?" It was David. "Stephen . . . my management's just gone to get the car." He pointed towards the car park. "You wanna talk about it?"

"Uhhh." My voice barely came out. My mouth was

dry. "Uhh . . . Yeah, I'm good." I squinted up at him, trying to avoid the sun hitting my eyes.

"You don't seem it." He sat down next to me and nudged my shoulder. "I saw you go to your brother for all of three seconds," he said.

Oh man. He was watching me the whole time!

"Didn't go well, then?"

"Not really . . ." I had to be honest.

"And why do you think it's his fault that you haven't seen your dad?"

I shrugged. "It just is." I knew I sounded stupid, but I felt like I had nothing to lose after looking like such an idiot fighting with my half brother.

David sighed. "It took me years to get used to Joe . . ."

I looked up at him. He had such a kind face. I wished in that moment *he* was my big brother.

"It took me years because when I was carrying around all that anger about my dad and his son, I was only hurting myself. But when I finally took the step to chat to him, and we got to know each other, I realized that my brother didn't choose to live with my dad. He didn't tell my dad to leave. He was just a young kid who needed a dad as much as me."

Something relaxed in me when he said that. As if something inside unlocked. Mustafa was just a kid too. It wasn't Mustafa's fault that my dad didn't see me. That was Dad's decision. *Dad* was the one who walked away. *He* was the one who didn't care. And he had just swanned through life as if it didn't matter.

I knew then that there was only one way I was ever going to be able to move on and never think of him again.

It would be hard.

But I had to do it.

Chapter 25

*D*ad *came out of the shop smiling,* holding loads of chocolate. My favorite, chocolate buttons, and lots of Kit Kats, almost spilling out of his hands. Did he get them for me?

How did he know?

Dad smiled. "I've missed you, Ali. You wanna kick a ball about? Spend some time together?"

My spine tingled, and I accidentally smiled. I couldn't help it.

"I heard you've been practicing penalty shoot-outs. Shall we do that? I'll get in goal if you want?"

"Yeah, okay," I said, following him to his car.

At the park, I put the ball on the ground and stepped back. If someone had told me I'd be playing football with my dad, I'd have laughed in their face. This was so weird.

I looked at the right goalpost and then the left, then booted the ball hard. The ball went over the net and landed somewhere in the hedges. Dad's smile dropped and he crossed his arms.

My knees felt weak. I hunched my shoulders in shame and jogged past him to get the ball. Dad tapped his foot, waiting for me to go and grab it.

As I made my way back onto the pitch, I noticed Dad's face had lit up. I looked to where he was focused. Mustafa was strolling over.

Oh, great.

"Shall I take the next shot?' Mustafa said.

I stepped back and watched.

He chipped the ball right into the back of the net. Dad beamed with pride and walked out of goal, putting his arm around Mustafa. "I'm so proud of you and so glad you're my son."

Mustafa smiled. "Shall we get some pizza?"

"Yeah, let's do that."

They walked off, so I followed. When Dad turned, his smile dropped and his face soured. "You can't come. There's no room for you." He glanced at Mustafa and rubbed his shoulders. They both walked off into the blazing sun.

I squinted, watching their silhouettes, then squeezed my eyes when the glare got too much.

Something hit my leg.

"Come on, we're gonna be late!"

I opened my eyes. It looked like a blurry Samira, my sis.

"If you don't get up now, I'm picking up my mates and then there'll be no room for you and your charity stuff in the car."

"Huh?" I looked around my bedroom and breathed out. I'd been sleeping. I didn't play football with Dad. And he didn't just reject me and walk off with Mustafa.

This was next level. He'd already invaded my thoughts, and now he was in my dreams, even when he had *nothing* to do with my life.

"Come on!" Samira put her head round the door again. "You've got to load the drinks too!" Mum had bought a huge box of juice cartons for the penalty shoot-out and asked Samira to drop me at school with them today.

I threw my duvet off and put my feet on the carpet,

hanging my head between my legs. I felt like I'd run for miles and needed a rest. Was this what stress felt like?

"All right!"

I stood up. How was I going to get through school feeling like this?

We gathered back at mine after school with Aadam to figure out how much we'd raised in ticket sales so far. Sami's dad had collected the money from Mrs. Webster yesterday, and Sami had begged him to drop it off to mine after school. He'd agreed when Sami had told him they were more likely to get robbed in his area. Mum was letting us count it out, and then she was going to keep it in her lockbox in her wardrobe until Sami's dad could get it deposited into his bank account.

"I've got three hundred pounds." I held out a wad of fivers, and Sami and Mark looked up from the coffee table midcount.

This was one of the most exciting things we'd done together and made up for the rubbish day I'd had, because Mr. Clarke had given me a detention at lunchtime for going after Mustafa like an idiot yesterday.

I blinked hard to get the cringey memory out of my head. One of the few times I actually lost it and did something *super* stupid, I got caught. And not just by anyone . . . By one of the best goalkeepers in the world. Ugh.

I guess I was lucky everyone had either gone home, was busy queuing for tickets around the corner, or was playing football, and no one on the pitch near enough to see us had their phones to record it. Especially Nathan.

Although if Nathan had seen David, that would've been awesome. I'm sure his face would've been perfect for a "no way this is happening" meme.

"I've counted eight hundred pounds!" Sami grinned as he wrote down the figure in his notebook.

I'd never seen so much cash in my life. Since word had got out David had turned up at school, *everyone* wanted a ticket and we'd sold out on Tuesday.

"Add my three hundred to that, and it's one thousand, one hundred pounds!" I said.

Sami's grin dropped. "That's nowhere near the target." We still needed so much more.

But Aadam didn't seem to care. He started recording a WhatsApp message in Arabic into his phone. His smile was as wide as his face, and you could hear the joy oozing out of his voice.

"Never seen him this happy," whispered Sami, looking at him. "He's telling his mum his lawyer has sent in the appeal application and his friends are helping him raise money for the fees and she shouldn't worry, he'll be safe and not put in a detention center. Although we better raise more, and soon." Sami tapped his foot as he put the cash back into the chocolate tub.

"We do still have spectator tickets. That will bring in at least another thousand pounds," said Mark. "Wait . . . we should do *two* penalty sessions to get more people involved and raise even more money!" Mark typed something on his phone. "It's my mum," he said, holding it up. "Just telling her I'm with Grace."

Mum knocked on the open door holding a tray full of small Pringles tubs, cookies, and cans of fizzy drinks. "I'm so proud of you boys," she said, putting the tray on the coffee table next to the money tub before leaving us to it.

The vibe in the room was good, and I knew I should be happy too, but I couldn't get rid of the sinking feeling I'd had since deciding what I needed to do about

Dad. I just couldn't work out *how* to do it. I picked up the remote control to find a show that might drown out my thoughts, but something deep inside me itched to do something now. Should I go to his house? Message him? I picked up my phone—

"Oi, Ali!"

I looked up.

"Clean your ears out, man!" said Mark. "Been calling you for about a minute."

"Eh? Serious? I didn't hear a thing."

"Where's the other PlayStation controllers? There's only two here." Mark had both in his hands and was crouched in front of the TV.

"Uhhh... Ahmed might've taken the extras upstairs. Hang on..." I slipped my phone into my pocket and went into the hallway. "Ahmed!" I shouted from the foot of the stairs. "Get me the extra two PlayStation controllers!"

Ahmed came out of our bedroom and leaned over the banister. "I dunno where they are!" He frowned.

"I swear you're mincemeat if you're lying!" I gritted my teeth to show him I wasn't messing about. I had no patience for him anymore. Little brothers were a waste of space.

"I'll have a look," he said, blinking. He turned back to our room.

He came halfway down the stairs with the controllers. The little liar. I reached up and grabbed them from his shaking hand. "So you did know where they were, you little—"

"I forgot!" He ran back up the stairs and slammed our bedroom door.

He seemed scared, and I was glad. I wanted to come across as scary and untouchable as possible.

Aadam and Mark were already playing a game. I handed Sami a controller and sat next to Aadam with the other.

"Go on, Aadam!" I said, as he took a tight corner in *Gran Turismo*. His engine roared as he sped off, leaving Mark behind.

"How are you good at everything?" Sami asked with his mouth open.

Aadam winked and focused on the screen.

I pulled out my phone again and started typing. I wasn't going to think about it this time. I was just going to do it.

> A: Salaam Dad. How are you?

Nah. That sounded stupid. I didn't really care how he was. And I didn't want to call him Dad and make his day. I deleted the line and started again.

> A: Salaam. I'm in Year 8

He didn't care about that. I deleted and started again.

> A: Salaam. Do you play football?

That was enough to start a conversation without me sounding desperate, right? I pressed send and put the phone next to my leg, so I'd see it light up when he replied.

"YEAHHH!" Aadam raised his arms over his head, celebrating his win.

"All right, now we play *FIFA*, see how you are there," said Mark, pulling the game out of the disc wallet.

"Yeah, I show you!" Aadam laughed.

We all chose our players, and I picked up my phone to see if Dad had replied. Nothing. But it said "read" under my message, which meant he'd seen it.

Mark started the game and off we went.

"Ali, what's happened to you, man? How'd you miss that kick!" said Sami, his eyes fixed on the TV.

I quickly put my phone down. I couldn't focus. My body felt heavy, and my heart felt like it was shriveling up inside. I'd decided I was gonna do this so I could move on, but now I'd only gone and made a fool of myself. I just wanted to tell him what he'd done. And how much he'd hurt us.

I tutted—I should've just left it up to him to make the effort. He was my dad—it wasn't up to me to make the first move!

I folded my arms tight across my chest and leaned back into the sofa.

"What you doin'?" asked Sami, glancing over while trying to keep his player dribbling the ball.

"I can't play," I said. "Got a pain in my chest." And I wasn't lying.

Sami dropped his controller and got up to look at me. Aadam turned, and Mark too.

"S'right. Just carry on. Think I need to sleep it off." I put my head back and closed my eyes. I needed to think of a time when there was no Dad and I never lashed out in anger because of him. That's the Ali I had to bring back.

Chapter 26

Running around the football pitch in the rain at lunchtime the next day, going hard at whoever had the ball, wasn't helping me the way I thought it would. But I didn't stop. Leo passed the ball to Elijah, who passed it to me. I took it and dribbled it around Tom. When he tackled me and won the ball, I went in to get it back with such force I kicked him in the shin. But I still didn't stop. I wanted to score. I set off with the ball and kicked it to Sami. He knew I'd run and he'd pass it back. But Nathan intercepted. So I went for him, and as he saw me closing in, he lunged, pushing me in my ribs, hard. I slipped on the wet grass and fell on my side, skidding across the pitch just as someone else went in to tackle Nathan. His boot made contact with my chin on the way up.

"Aaaaargh!" I screamed, putting my hand to the searing pain on my chin. It felt like it had split apart. Blood oozed all over my hands and shirt.

Everyone gathered round, and Sami held out his hand to help me up.

"Mark! Come here!" shouted Sami. "Put your arm around my shoulder," he said to me, and nodded at Mark, who leaned down to support me on the other side.

"I can walk. I haven't hurt my legs," I groaned, in pain as I cupped my chin to collect the blood pouring from it. Mark put his arm around my back, and they both walked me across the field.

"Just put me on that bench. I'll be all right." I winced.

" . . . no, you're going to the nurse," said Sami.

"I don't need to, man!"

"Mate, you ain't seen your chin, have you?" said Mark.

I scowled and let them take me to the medical room.

"Oh, that's a cut if I ever did see one," said the school nurse, squatting to get right under my chin to look at it.

Mark and Sami stood in the doorway looking in. Mark was biting his nails, and Sami was twisting his shirt button repeatedly. He seemed distressed—the blood might have triggered some bad memories of what he'd seen in Syria, but I couldn't say anything with the nurse's face under my chin.

I looked around the bland room and took it all in—the posters, the desk and computer, the dull cupboards, the manky bed . . . I hoped the nurse wouldn't make me lie down on it. Did they even change the sheets? I'd never seen anyone carrying laundry or folded sheets in the school. The nurse got up and opened a cupboard door.

"Can I go and finish off the match, Miss?" I asked.

"Football?" The school nurse knelt down, putting her gloves on. Then she peeled back the plastic from a sealed square blood-clotting bandage, put the dry cloth on my chin, and held it there.

I winced. "Yeah."

"Well, let's see if I can glue this together, otherwise you'll need stitches."

"Stitches?"

"Yep. Just hold still. It looks like we might be able to avoid them . . . Let me clean you up properly and then we'll see."

She put a cold, damp antiseptic wipe onto my cut and swiped.

I squeezed my eyes shut, keeping my head as still as possible as she wiped some more, trying to ignore the stinging even though I wasn't feeling brave right then.

"Right, close your mouth and be as still as possible. I'm going to try and skin-glue this. If it works, you won't need stitches," she said, before squeezing together what must've been the two parts of my skin that had split open. The pressure felt good, and I hoped the glue would keep it like that.

I held my breath to stop myself from moving as she applied something sticky that smelled like a sweet chemical. She stepped back. "Hmm, good. You were lucky it was a pretty straightforward cut." She turned to the cabinets behind her and opened a drawer, then pulled out a big bandage and some scissors and some other things I couldn't see.

"I'm going to apply some steri strips, to hold it together." She cut the long strips into halves and applied three. Then she peeled the back of the big bandage off and stuck it onto my chin. "There. Keep this on all day, please. I've put it there so you don't touch the glue or strips. But you'll have to keep an eye on it. If it starts bleeding through the strips or feels sore or painful, or you get a temperature, you'll need go to the hospital for stitches."

"Okay," I said, glancing at Mark and Sami, who were still standing in the doorway watching.

"Oh, and you've got to keep the wound dry for at least five days—"

"Five days!" I said. "How am I meant to shower?"

"You can wash your body." The nurse pushed her foot down on the pedal of a bin and threw away all the rubbish. "Just not your hair. And you can't put your face in the shower—use a wet cloth around the steri strips instead." She peeled back her gloves and tossed them before turning the tap on and squeezing foamy soap onto her hands.

The fundraiser was in just over a week. What if we bumped into David? Was I meant to meet him with my hair smelling like rubbish?

Everything was going wrong because I just couldn't control my feelings. First, I'd taken it out on Mustafa, then I'd been nasty to Ahmed and tried to scare him, and then I'd done some really dangerous tackles like I was Nathan or something. It was as if the rage inside me couldn't be contained anymore. I was erupting like a volcano and all the lava was spilling out and burning my family, my friends, my teammates. It served me right that Nathan had gone for me. I'd asked for it.

I wished Dad hadn't come back. He'd upset the balance and ruined the life we'd built without him.

He needed to know.

And I was going to tell him.

He hadn't replied to my message, so I'd have to find another way. No more thinking about it.

"There you go!" The nurse handed me a fresh bandage and some more steri strips. "Just in case you need to reapply tonight."

"Thanks." I got up.

"Right, Ali," said the nurse at her computer. "Make sure you rest. Avoid any activities that'll make the cut split again . . . like football." She gave me a look and then went back to typing something on her keyboard. "Okay? I'll give your mum a call."

"Yeah. Thanks, Miss."

"Oh, and keep it dry!" she said as we all headed out into the corridor.

Mustafa was leaning against the wall outside the medical room. He glanced at my chin, nodded, and walked off. Just like that.

I forced myself to nod at him so that he knew I

didn't hate him after my stupid behavior the other day. Why was he here?

"You think he came to check on you?" said Sami, watching Mustafa open the door and leave the building.

"Nah," I said, but I wondered if he had. Why else would he be outside and then walk off as soon as he'd seen me?

It wasn't Mustafa's fault that Dad only loved him. But still, I was going to make sure I didn't have to see him or our dad anymore.

They had no right to just come back as if nothing had happened. A whole lot had happened. And it didn't include them.

Chapter 27

*T*he throbbing on my chin had gone and the steri strips from the day before were still intact. I'd even managed to keep it all dry. Apart from the odd twinge, it was pretty much feeling normal, even though *I* still wasn't.

It was a warm afternoon, and with exactly a week to go to the shoot-out, I'd decided to walk Sami home so we could chat about it. When we got to his house, I could just make out their gleaming door number in the bright sunlight.

Sami put the key in his front door. "You coming in?"

"Nah," I replied quickly. "I've gotta head back. Mum wants me to do something for her." I shuffled my feet and looked down, hoping Sami wouldn't detect my lies. I didn't want to tell him what I was actually thinking of doing.

"Oh, Ali! How are you?" I looked up to find Sami's dad standing in the doorway.

"Good, thanks, Uncle," I said.

"What are you doing home, Dad?" said Sami.

"Came home to spend some time with you!" His dad smiled and put his arms out to hug Sami.

My teeth clenched, and my chest felt like it was on fire. I looked away, hoping Sami wouldn't see my eyes had turned green or whatever. There was no way I could hide how his dad saying that made me feel. I hated this. I'd been fine about his dad being around before. Why couldn't I just get on with it now?

I pulled my phone out and pretended to look at a message.

"No . . . really, why are you here, Dad?" Sami laughed.

"I forgot some papers . . ." His dad sounded sheepish. "Come in, Ali. I've got some fresh maamoul, stuffed with the best dates. Come have some."

I had to look at him.

I shoved my phone into my pocket. "Errr . . . thanks, Uncle, but I can't. My mum wants me home."

"Okay, well, let us know when you're coming next and I'll make sure we have some more."

"Thanks. I will," I said, looking at them both standing in the doorway, before turning to leave. "See you tomorrow, Sami."

"See ya!" He smiled.

I got out my phone again as I walked off, opening my map app. Just one left turn and another left . . . so close . . .

I got to the end of Sami's road and stood at the junction. *Turn right to go home, or you could go left . . .*

I took a deep breath. So this was where he lived. I stepped forward and put my fist to the white plastic door, giving it a firm knock. My brain had let my legs take over. It was done thinking about what I should do and had let my body decide. I stood back to look at the house. All this time, my own dad was living on the same council estate as Sami, only a block away, and I, his own son, had no idea.

I rolled my neck as if I was a boxer preparing for a fight. I was going to tell my dad he was a loser and that I wanted nothing to do with him. If he had any decency, he'd leave the area and leave me alone forever instead of pushing his loseriness in my face every day.

The door opened.

I swallowed, then blew out, ready to go for it.

Dad walked forward . . . holding a baby in his arms.

I stepped back and felt my brows stretch to my hairline.

"I—I—I . . ." I didn't know what to say.

So now I had *another* sibling? WHAT?!

"Oh, Ali! I wasn't expecting you! Come . . . come in," said Dad, gesturing me inside.

Time slowed down, and it felt as if Dad was speaking in slo-mo. I watched him wave me in and turn to go inside. But I just stood there, my insides feeling empty. I could run off right now and pretend this never happened, or I could go in and see how this man—my dad—lived. I gave a half-hearted shrug and exhaled before taking what felt like the biggest step of my life.

Dad stood in the narrow hallway. "This is your baby sister . . . I used to cradle you like this too." He patted the baby's back and walked into the living room.

I had no idea he'd cradled me. It felt like he'd never really been there when I was growing up. He was always out. I probably had three memories of him, and they might've been from the photos I'd seen.

"Sit, sit." Dad pointed at the beat-up black leather three-seater next to his equally battered armchair. "What happened to your chin?" He stared at the bandage covering it.

"Uhhh . . . it's just a cut."

He nodded and didn't seem to want to know more. What a surprise.

The house smelled of rice and was dark. The walls were painted a pale mint, and the floor was a plasticky old laminate, like we used to have before Ahmed slipped on it, landed on the coffee table corner, and cracked his chin open. I realized we'd both done it now. Although Mum had to take him to the hospital and he'd had proper stitches.

A floorboard creaked above us, and I looked up. The ceiling had water stains, and the windows were grimy. Mum would totally tell him to open them and get some fresh air in.

The clock ticked, and I sat with my hands between my legs, wondering if I should get up again or get on and say what I needed to. A pipe gurgled, and then water started running. Someone was having a shower upstairs. Maybe Dad's wife. It was Friday, so Mustafa would be at Year Seven football training.

Dad stared at me as he patted the baby, who was gawping at the wall behind him.

"What was I like as a baby, then?" *Let's see if he actually knows anything.*

"Oh, you were a handful." He laughed. "One time we couldn't find you, and we looked everywhere. Under the bed, in the wardrobes, in the kitchen cabinets—and you'd only gone and run off outside, barefoot, in your nappy and managed to get an ice lolly from the ice-cream-van man!" He laughed from his chest and then started coughing.

I smiled. I knew this story. Mum had told it to me too.

He came across like he was a good dad and as if he'd been present. And he looked like he was a good dad now, so what happened?

It was now or never. I had to tell him what him leaving had done to us . . . to me.

"You know, I thought you were amazing." I glared at the blank TV as I spoke. "I remember when you took me to town and we both wore a white shirt and jeans and I was on top of the world. Just me and my dad.

There's a photo of that day in our album too. But you forgot about me. You didn't even look back. Until you had to, because your perfect son now goes to my school."

"Hey, Ali! It's not like that!" Dad shuffled to the edge of his armchair, his mouth hanging open. "Listen, please. Of course I thought of you. And I made dua for you all every day but I just couldn't face coming back after the way I left. And the longer I left it, the harder it got. So I just buried my head in the sand and stayed away and focused on my new family . . ."

He put his head down.

"And I know that was wrong. Look, Ali, I know I've got a lot of making up to do. But I'm here right now. So give me a chance?"

I said nothing. I couldn't understand the part where he just didn't bother. That's not what love is. When you love someone, apparently, you'd do anything for them. Like Mum—she never abandoned us, no matter how hard it got. And Sami's family wasn't even related to Aadam, but they were always there for him. Dad never loved us like that. He'd taught me there was a big difference between real love and his fake version.

"Errr . . . I better go," I said, quickly getting up.

"But you just got here! Let me get you a drink at least!"

"No, I have an after-school club to go to," I lied. "I was passing by and just thought I'd see where you lived."

Dad stood up with the baby still over his shoulder and put his hand in his pocket. He grabbed my arm, and once he had my attention, he pushed a ten-pound note into my hand. "I'm sorry I went missing. But I'm here now, and we can make up for it?"

My arms dropped to my sides, and my stomach hardened. Was this what I wanted? Because, having heard it, I wasn't sure it was.

Chapter 28

The next day, the sun was shining, the summer vibe was strong, and me and Sami didn't want to go home just yet after playing football in the park, so we decided to ride back with Mark on our bikes.

Sami looked around, anxious Callum might see us, but for some reason I wasn't bothered. He didn't own the street, so he couldn't really kick up a fuss if we didn't step onto his drive.

An old man in a checked suit stepped out of his side gate with a white poodle on a lead. He looked at us as if we were trouble. We rode faster towards Mark's house so the man would know we had a reason to be here. We stopped on the road outside, making sure we weren't anywhere near Mark's driveway.

Mark climbed off his bike and turned to us. We heard a whirr and clack, and the gates outside David's house started opening.

And my heart started racing.

His Porsche's engine purred as the beautiful red car emerged.

David smiled at us and then pushed his shades up onto his head. "How you doing, boys? All set for the shoot-out next week?"

"Yeah!" we all said together.

"We've sold out of our tickets!" said Sami with his whole chest.

Mark walked onto his driveway and leaned his bike on the wall. "Actually, we were wondering if we should have two shoot-outs 'cause we haven't raised as much as we need to but we weren't sure if that's doable."

David stared at Mark. "You mean, two separate shoot-outs on the same day?"

"Yeah, so more people can join in and it means you can have a break in between," said Mark.

"*And* we can sell more tickets that way," Sami said. "I worked out if we can do six penalties a minute, we could sell three hundred and sixty tickets. And at five pounds each, that's . . ."

"One thousand eight hundred pounds," David finished off for Sami. He looked at me and I shuffled my feet. He might've been wondering why I wasn't talking, but I didn't know what to say. Or if I *should* say anything, after the other day.

"Yeah, sure. It's for a good cause. But you'll have to speak to your head teacher about logistics and that. There's no way we can do six penalties a minute if you include time to collect balls, place balls, and me getting up after each dive! But let's try and get as many in as we can manage." David smiled. "We could have a break after the first shoot-out and then do an extra half hour. I could definitely do that." He put his hands on his steering wheel, and the silver on his watch face glistened. "I'll see you boys next week!" He locked eyes with me, then nodded before turning right and driving off.

He'd looked right at me! And nodded! I felt like my chest was going to tear my shirt, like the Hulk . . . but not because I was angry. I felt special . . . supported . . . seen. He understood what it felt like to be rejected. And David was living proof you could be successful even if you didn't have a dad in your life. Maybe if he could do it, then I could too.

I didn't need my dad; I knew that. And I didn't

need him to *see* me. I just had to see myself, like David had. He had believed in himself. And that's what I needed to do.

The speaker on the gate started screeching. I looked at Mark and Sami. Mark's eyes flitted around in a panic.

"Don't worry," I said, climbing onto my bike. "We're off!"

Sami stood up from his saddle and started pedaling away. I turned to nod at Mark before following Sami.

I hoped Mark's mum and Callum wouldn't go too hard on Mark.

Once we got near Sami's house, we got off our bikes, wheeling them and walking.

"What's going on with you, Ali?" asked Sami. "You've been different lately."

"No, I haven't," I replied quickly.

"Yes, you have. You're angry. You don't laugh anymore. Haven't heard you make a joke in ages. You were playing football like Nathan does the other day, and then you got hurt. And you're not really with us even when you're sitting with us. Your head is always somewhere else." He glanced at me for a moment. "Is it your dad and Mustafa?"

I looked at Sami, who was now focused ahead. It

was weird how the roles had reversed. I had been the one who was always looking out for Sami and making sure he was okay. But now Sami was doing it for me.

"Not gonna lie," I finally said, and Sami glanced at me again. Think he'd given up on me answering. Maybe he could tell I was lost in thought. "It's been hard to see my dad around."

"You know, sometimes you can have a parent who is there but isn't, really."

"You mean your dad?"

"Yeah." Sami looked down.

Even though Sami's dad was around, he was so busy trying to rebuild their lives, Sami barely saw him. Even that day he was home, he was only there to pick up some papers.

"I know it isn't the same," said Sami, knocking my elbow. "But I've had issues with my dad too, and I just wanted you to know I get it."

I wasn't sure if he did. Being the rejected one was definitely worse. But I didn't want to say anything. Sami just trying to be there for me was enough.

Chapter 29

That night, my phone buzzed on the bedside table. I looked across the room to see if it'd woken Ahmed, then picked it up to find a message from Dad. At ten o'clock on a Saturday night?

> D: Can I take you and Ahmed out after school on Monday?

I lay back on my pillow and closed my eyes.

I didn't want to go out with Dad, but I couldn't make the decision for Ahmed. I had to give him the option before I said no. Although if I didn't go and he did, that'd just make me look bad.

Feeling around on the bedside table, I turned to put my phone back next to our shared alarm clock. Ahmed lay in his bed with his back to me. I watched his body rise and fall. He had no idea what Dad was like. He'd had even less time with him than me. Did he think about Dad the way I did? Especially since he'd found out Dad had moved back? I turned onto my back and stared at the ceiling. The streetlight filtered in above the curtain rail, allowing me to make out the glow-in-the-dark stars that had been Ahmed's reward for getting potty-trained when he turned three. They'd been up there since. Dad hadn't even been there for that.

When Ahmed scrambled out of bed the next morning, I pretended to sleep but watched him through slitted eyes. I hadn't slept all night, worrying about having to hang out with Dad. I'd been through every option, and each one ended in a catastrophe with either me and Ahmed sitting in absolute, awkward silence with nothing to say; or Dad talking *nonstop* and us not understanding a word; or me walking off in a huff halfway through because I couldn't handle Dad being all fatherly with Mustafa; or Dad walking off; or me and Mustafa lobbing food at each other in anger, leading to a fistfight; or me and Dad doing that (I wished I could chuck tomatoes at him); or the worst of all, Dad telling me he was glad he'd never made the effort to see us before and that seeing us now had confirmed that he'd made the right decision when he'd abandoned us.

Ahmed pulled open the curtains. "Gerr up!"

"Shut your Year Six mouth!" I said, trying to keep things normal.

"You had a nightmare last night," he said, pulling off his pajama top over his bushy bed hair. "You were proper yelling."

"Seriously?" I thought I hadn't slept at all. "What was I shouting?"

"Something about Dad." He ripped off his pajama trousers and walked to the door in his red-and-white stripy boxers. "I know you saw him." He looked at me and I sat up. "Mum told me. She said I can meet up with him too."

I let my shoulders drop and sighed. "Hang on, don't go," I said. Ahmed stopped at the door. "Dad messaged me last night. Said he wants to take us both out tomorrow after school but I—"

"Yessss!" Ahmed's face lit up. The complete opposite to how mine felt, dull and stiff. "Where we goin'?"

I blew out a long breath. "Not sure, I haven't replied yet."

"Well, what you waitin' for?" He looked at me and then at my phone.

I guess I had to do this.

But I was dreading it.

At school on Monday we got harassed as soon as we got through the gates. Kids wanted tickets "to play against David," and it seemed they didn't understand what "we need more time to get things sorted" meant. Mark had spoken to Mrs. Webster and got permission to print more tickets for the extra penalty shoot-out, but we still needed to cut them, and it felt too long to explain that to each kid.

As the gazillionth kid approached me, Sami, and Mark, Nathan walked past, staring us out. If looks could kill, I'd have keeled over and died right then.

"Please, me and my mates need five," said a tiny Year Seven with a floppy boy-band haircut. Even Ahmed was taller than him.

Then another kid came and joined him, and

another. I let Sami and Mark deal with them and just stood there. I didn't trust myself not to mess things up again.

"Look, we'll let you know as soon as they're ready, yeah? Don't worry, you won't miss out," said Mark, turning his back to them.

The kids walked away, and Mark leaned in, adjusting his rucksack and putting his phone back in his blazer pocket. "Grace is gonna buy a ticket to come and watch, so I was thinking we could let her buy a penalty shoot-out ticket. I mean, she is Mrs. Hack's daughter and she did come and support our games."

"I dunno," I said. "We could ask Mrs. Hack? Then it's legit too."

"Yeah, that makes sense," said Mark.

By the end of school, tickets for the second penalty session had already sold out. And we'd printed extra spectators' ones, which were selling fast at two pounds. Word was spreading—if the excitement in the playground was anything to go by, we'd probably be sold out by tomorrow.

"We must've made thousands for Aadam's appeal now!" Mark said, following Sami through the school gates.

We all fist-bumped each other and grinned. I really hoped we'd made the target.

"Ali!" someone shouted from somewhere across the street. I looked around and spotted Dad waving . . . with Mustafa standing beside him.

My smile dropped. I'd forgotten me and Ahmed were supposed to meet him today. I wanted to run, but it was as if my brain was secretly telling my legs not to move.

A white car pulled up and hooted. The tinted windows came down on the front passenger side. Mark's mum.

"Get in the car now, Mark!"

"I thought I was walking home today!" he said, his cheeks looking warm.

"Get 'ere now! I told you not to hang out with those thugs!"

Thugs?!

"You what?" Dad marched up to Mark's mum's car. "What did you just call my son?"

Whoa. His son? Did he just call me his son? I felt my chest swelling, and suddenly I felt taller.

Mark's mum's eyes almost popped out. I don't think she was expecting an adult to confront her. "Oh, I wasn't talking about your son or anyone in particular."

"I better go." Mark glanced at us. He got in the car, and as soon as he'd pulled the door shut, his mum sped off.

Dad stood exactly where he'd just been shouting at Mark's mum and looked at me, shaking his head.

I couldn't help but smile.

Chapter 30

The date with Dad was as awkward as I'd expected. From having to crawl into the back seat of the car *behind* Mustafa, who sat in the front, and trying not to choke because of the strong aftershave Dad was wearing to Ahmed acting like an excited puppy dog, practically panting over Dad AND Mustafa when we picked him up from school. I sat in silence, facing forward, with my hands on my lap, as if I was at a new auntyji's house and didn't understand the language.

Mustafa stared at his phone the whole way. Dad listened to the radio, where weirdos were calling in and complaining about the government not doing enough to keep refugees out, and Ahmed, after a few minutes, realized we weren't going to be chatting, so he stared out the window gripping the door panel.

AWKWARD.

Dad took us to the Pizza Hut in the Trafford Centre. It was obvious we had nothing in common from what they chose at the salad bar. They both chose the lettuce. It wasn't on their plates because it happened to be *with* their food; they actually picked shredded lettuce up with the tongs! Wrong.

Mustafa sat next to Dad in the booth, while me and Ahmed sat opposite them. I shifted in my seat, unsure what to say, and tried not to make eye contact with Dad. It just didn't feel right to be here with him and Mustafa. They didn't feel like family.

A waiter came and handed Ahmed the kids' menu. He didn't even notice it as he'd gone all googly-eyed at his shiny new half brother and Dad. So I pulled the sheet and the cup of crayons towards me and started filling in the activities.

"Do you play *Minecraft*?" Ahmed asked while Dad read the menu.

"Yeah, do you?" Mustafa put his menu down and leaned in to the table.

"We should friend each other, then we can hang out in our games!" Ahmed's voice was so high-pitched, it hurt my ears.

They started chatting about one of their games like little kids at primary school. I tried my best not to roll my eyes while Dad looked at them both as if all his dreams had come true. I could just as easily have not been there and no one would've noticed.

After we'd eaten, Dad rushed us out of our seats, telling us he had to go somewhere. I was secretly hoping we'd walk around the shopping center and he'd take me to JD Sports to buy some new trainers, but nope, our date was the pizza and chat about school and straight back to the car. We weren't good enough for anything more.

Ahmed nodded off pretty much as soon as we left the car park. Mustafa put his earbuds in, and Dad put on the radio, listening to callers now moaning about the royal family, so I replied to Sami's and Mark's messages on our group chat.

The penalty shoot-out was in four days, and they wanted to meet up tomorrow for a game of *FIFA* and to count the last of the ticket money so we could check how many more spectator tickets we had to sell. Even though we'd sold out the penalty tickets for both shoot-outs, I didn't think we'd made the full four-thousand-pound target. If we didn't, would Aadam's new application be canceled? I think we'd all tried to avoid that conversation for too long, pretending everything was going well, but now we had to have it. I started typing:

> A: Come round to mine. I'll be home in half an hour.

Sami was up for it, and Mark said he'd see if he could meet Grace later instead.

"Thanks," I said to Dad as I squeezed out the back seat and jumped onto the street.

"So this is where you lived?" Mustafa said to Dad, staring at our house as he held his seat forward to let Ahmed out.

I watched Mustafa taking it all in. And it hit me again that he was struggling too. While I'd been focusing on Dad's life right now, with him, he was thinking about Dad's previous life in this house. With us.

I made my way up our short drive, waiting for Ahmed to scramble out. Ahmed waved at them, and Dad waved back before driving off.

My muscles finally relaxed, now that I'd got away.

I breathed out.

It was over. Thank God.

I put the key in the front door, hoping Mum

wouldn't come home any minute now. She'd want to know everything, and I didn't really want to diss our date in front of Ahmed, who looked like he'd just had a massive birthday party and been given the best present ever. And even though she'd encouraged us to go out with Dad, it just felt awkward to have spent time with the man who had let her down big-time. Man, this whole thing was just so confusing. A mess.

The boys got to mine about twenty minutes after we'd got home. I handed them a PlayStation controller each as they sat down.

"How was it?" asked Sami, biting his lip.

"Fine," I said, staring at the TV screen as I loaded the game. "Just pizza and back home."

Mark shifted in his seat. Dads were an awkward conversation for him too. Between his dad passing away a long time ago and now all the stuff with Callum, I bet it was a lot to handle.

"Hey, let's present Aadam with the money after the penalty shoot-out!" he said. "One of those big fancy checks."

Thanks for changing the conversation, I thought.

"Uhhh . . . I don't think we can do that," said Sami, looking serious.

"Why not?" I asked.

"Aadam's really shy. He'd hate to get up in front of hundreds of people to be given money. Plus, the school is giving the final amount to my dad tomorrow."

"Ah, okay," I said. "Hey, what you gonna tell your mum when you get home and she asks where you've been?" I mean, Mark's mum had called us thugs just a few hours ago!

Mark shrugged. "I'm gonna tell her I was here. She needs to know."

"You sure?" I said.

"Yep."

I fist-bumped him, and Sami got up to lean over me and bump him.

A proper bro moment.

What a day.

Why was I worrying about my weird dad and weird half brother when I had my boys by my side? I'd always been good enough for them. I had to remember that.

Chapter 31

The evening was still light and warm, and we had no homework, so we decided to bike home with Mark. We turned in to the quiet, empty, tree-lined road and headed down the middle, instead of along the grass verges that bordered all the big gates to the mansions.

A blackbird sat in one of the trees ahead of us and sang loud. It sounded like Grace wolf whistling. I turned around, just to make sure she wasn't behind us. She wasn't. It was just the pretty and peaceful road stretching behind us.

"So we'll be there when school gives Aadam and your dad the last of the money tomorrow, yeah?" Mark said to Sami, riding with one hand in his pocket.

"Yeah, he's gonna be so happy."

"We can take photos, right?" I asked, tapping my phone in my blazer pocket, and at the same time wondering if I had any messages from Dad.

"Yeah, I think so!" said Sami. He climbed off his bike as Mark rode up his driveway.

I stayed on my bike and pulled out my phone. There weren't any new messages. I slipped it back into my pocket.

"All right, thanks for riding with me. You gonna get the bus back or ride the whole way?" said Mark, punching in the code to the front gate.

"Yeah, probably get the bus. It'll be quicker," I said.

"See you at school, then," said Sami, trying to peek through the gates.

An engine revved down the street behind us. I rode my bike onto Mark's driveway and stepped off, then leaned it on the wall next to Sami's. We all looked back just as a white Range Rover stopped on the driveway. Oh man. Not again.

The massive front gates started opening, but Callum jumped out of the front passenger door. Me and Sami stepped back, closer to the pedestrian gate on the side. My heart started racing. Mark's mum stared at us through her sunglasses and then drove through the gate. Callum watched the car pass. I put my hands in my pockets, unsure what to do. Then he came at us, fast, and shoved his sneering face into mine.

"Get off my property." He scowled. "Otherwise, I'll break your legs so you can't step here again."

I tried not to inhale the stinky alcohol on his breath and stared him in the eye, unable to look away.

Mark ran forward. "Leave my friends alone!"

Callum put his finger in Mark's face. "*You* can't tell me what to do. You're not the man of the house. I am."

I swallowed. What were we supposed to do now?

Mark's face turned pink.

"Now get inside and help your mum with the shopping!"

Mark clenched his fists and stormed off through the gate before turning and saying, "Text me to let me know you got home safe!"

I nodded, noticing the sadness in his face.

"Now get outta here!" Callum shouted at me and Sami.

I flinched, then quickly grabbed my bike and

turned it onto the road, getting on it as I moved. Sami did the same.

"Should we call the police on him?" Sami asked as we slowed down a few houses along the road.

"What for? He didn't do anything."

"He threatened you."

"Yeah, but I didn't get hurt."

"True. I think he's dangerous though."

"Yeah, me too," I said. I just wanted to get off this road quickly now.

As we turned onto the main road, my phone started buzzing in my pocket.

It was Mark video-calling us on our group chat. I stopped riding to answer it, and Sami stopped too. What had happened? It must be urgent for him to be calling so soon after we left.

"It's Mark." I showed Sami the screen, and he nodded as if to say, "Answer it." We both got off our bikes at the corner.

"Oh my God, that was so embarrassing. I'm really sorry about him."

"It's not your fault!" both Sami and me said together.

We looked at each other and nudged shoulders.

"There's something seriously off about him," I said, watching Mark pacing his bedroom.

"Yeah, I know," said Mark. He put his knuckle in his mouth. He looked like he was thinking. After a second, he looked like he'd figured something out. "I'm sick of him. Did you hear him say 'my property,' as if he owns the house? I reckon he's got a plan to turn my mum against me."

"You think?" said Sami, his eyes wider and sadder than Simba's when his dad died in *The Lion King*.

"Yeah." Mark started pacing the floor again. "I can't let that happen. Mum can't see it for herself so I'm gonna have to prove to her that it wasn't Aadam that took the money. I've got to get rid of Callum once and for all." He started chewing on his knuckle and thinking again.

"Hang on!" I said, having a massive brain wave. "You said there's CCTV everywhere except the bedrooms, didn't you?!"

"Oh my God, yes, bro! Why the heck didn't I think of that before?"

"Maybe 'cause Aadam never went inside the house so we just didn't think it was relevant?" Sami's face had lit up like a lighthouse. "And we've been busy trying to organize the penalty shoot-out . . ."

And I'd got totally distracted by my dad turning up. But I didn't want to say it out loud.

"Oh, God!" Mark slapped his palm to his forehead. "And there should be recordings! I think they're kept for a month. I'll have to work out how to get to them though . . . Gonna google how to view CCTV now."

"Okay, so," I said, moving the phone as my arm was now aching from holding it up in front of our faces. "How can we help?"

But it didn't seem like Mark was listening anymore. "I've never liked Callum. He seemed bad from the start . . . What if he set Aadam up because he wanted to get rid of you guys? I've heard him rant racist stuff at the news and my mum *never* spoke like that till he came along and he added her to this weird group on Facebook."

"Yeah, she was nice to us!" said Sami, shoving his face into the screen.

"He's definitely tricked her into listening to him." Mark sat on the end of his bed. The oak headboard was as wide as the one we'd had in our hotel room on holiday.

"So where's the CCTV kept?" Sami asked.

"Uhhh . . . in one of the downstairs cupboards."

"Can you get into it without them seeing you?" I asked.

"Yeah, they're always going out. I might try tonight if they go to the pub."

"All right, well, let us know if you want us to help, yeah?" I said.

Mark fell back on his bed and held his phone above his face. "I will. But I'm sorry, yeah?"

"Mark, shut up. *He's* the idiot. We all know that," I said.

He gave a slight smile. "You guys get home. I'll message you later."

"All right, bye." I looked around and noticed there were fewer cars on the road now. We'd better get home before the sun set.

≋

The smell of lamb wafted through the hallway as I entered.

"Ali, you were gone ages!" Mum said as I slammed the door shut behind me and slipped out of my shoes.

"Yeah, sorry. We decided to ride to Mark's house

and it took ages to get a bus back because they don't come regularly after six o'clock."

"Well, don't go there so late in future, and answer your phone, okay?"

"I didn't wanna use all my data up if it wasn't urgent!"

"You don't use data when answering a phone, Ali! It wasn't a WhatsApp call!" She turned to go back into the kitchen. "Get washed and come and eat your dinner."

I walked into the front room, where Ahmed sat staring at the TV screen. "You still playin' baby games?" I said. "I was playin' *FIFA* at your age. Not *Minecraft*." I realized I was being mean to him again so added, "But . . . uhhh . . . you do you, lil' bro."

Ahmed ignored me and carried on walking his avatars all over the room he'd designed.

"Where's Samira?"

"Upstairs, I dunno," Ahmed grunted. I noticed Kinder egg foil next to his thigh.

"Oh, gimme some!" I said, picking it up as I sat down next to him.

Ahmed dropped his controller and snatched the foil back. "Don't!"

"Where's the chocolate? You ate it all?" I put my hand out to pick up the yellow plastic egg, and Ahmed blocked me.

"Don't touch it. Dad gave it me!" he said, grabbing it and holding it as if he'd won a massive prize.

I snorted. "What, is that all he's managed to get you after eleven years?" I sat back into the sofa.

Dad had got him something. He didn't get me *anything*.

"So what? It's the thought that counts."

"When'd he give it to you?" I asked.

"At Pizza Hut."

"What, when I was there?" My stomach hardened.

"You went to get more colors for the activity set . . . like a baby." Ahmed made a face.

He only thought of Ahmed. Maybe Dad just didn't like *me*. Who was I trying to kid? It was me after all.

My phone buzzed in my pocket, and I pulled it out. It was Mark.

I swiped to answer the call.

"Ali," Mark whispered.

"Yeah, you okay?" I glanced at Ahmed playing *Minecraft* again and got off the sofa to head upstairs.

"I found it . . . on the CCTV . . ."

"Found what?" I started climbing the stairs.

"I saw Callum in the boot room putting loads of cash—like wads of it—in Aadam's rucksack."

"What?" I stopped in the middle of the staircase.

"Yep. Now I've gotta find a way to show Mum the recording without him being there."

Chapter 32

*A*hmed pulled the curtains apart, and I sat up in bed. I stretched my arms and yawned, watching him leave the room in his school uniform. Man, it was too early to be getting up, and Ahmed was already dressed?! I was having a really good dream as well.

I picked up my phone from the bedside table and saw that Dad had messaged.

> **D:** Salaam Ali. I've had an idea. Speak to you today after school.

Ugh. I propped up my pillow and leaned back. What was this? Another way to get to Ahmed through me? I didn't really mean anything to him.

I swallowed. I had to stop thinking about Dad. I jumped out of bed and looked in the mirror. Had I had a growth spurt? I could swear I wasn't as tall as the hooks on the door last time I looked.

"Ali, wake up!" Mum shouted from downstairs.

"I'm up!" I yelled back. Mum. The parent who'd actually been there for me through everything. All my school assemblies, all the doctor's appointments, all the parents' evenings, and football matches. I was going to be extra nice to her today.

Yanking open the bedroom door made all the clothes I'd hung on the back of it sway.

"Ahmed!" I banged on the bathroom door. Trust him to go in when I needed a pee.

"He's down here!" Mum said from the foot of the stairs.

I looked through the spindles on the staircase and smiled at her. She watched me, puzzled, but smiled back.

In the kitchen, Mum handed me my cereal bowl. "Thanks, Mum," I said.

Samira tutted and rolled her eyes at Mum. "You spoil him sooo much." She took a sip of her coffee.

"'Cause I'm worth it." I grinned. "Why you here and not at uni?"

"Got an exam later." She took another sip. "And you're already late."

I glanced at the wall clock with my spoon half in my mouth. It was eight o'clock. Ugh. Sami would be here any minute now.

᠊᠊᠊

"Ali!" Mustafa shouted as I walked out the gate after school. "Over here!"

He stood across the road, next to Dad's car. I could just make out Dad's arm on the steering wheel through the open passenger window. It was weird how this all seemed so familiar now.

I looked at Sami, and he raised his brows as if to say, "Go."

"I'll wait here," he said.

I sighed deeply. "All right."

I pushed my hands into my pockets and looked left and right. Cars came down the road steadily, and then one stopped to let me cross. "Thanks!" I shouted, and rushed across.

Mustafa was now in the passenger seat. Dad's copilot. What did Dad even want?

I stepped in front of his open window. "As-salaamu Alaikum."

Dad looked up from tuning his radio and turned to me with a big smile. "Ah, Ali! Walaikum As-salaam. How are you?"

"Errr . . ." I put my hands in my pockets.

Thankfully, Dad didn't wait for a response. He put his bare arm on the windowsill and leaned towards me. "So, I had an idea about your charity thing."

I bent over and saw Mustafa doing something on his phone. Wow, so he was just letting Dad talk to me.

Dad continued. "Mustafa told me about it. If you want to make more money for this charity at the . . . the . . ."

"The penalty shoot-out." I completed his sentence for him.

"Yeah. You could print certificates for the people who go up against the footballer and they can pay if they want one to remember the moment by? I'm working at a local printing press so I can do them there for you."

"Oh, okay . . . ," I said, stepping back a little. I'd have to agree, because it was such a good idea and there was no way I could afford to get them printed myself.

"Maybe the footballer could sign them too? That would make the whole thing even more special."

"That's a really good idea!" I couldn't help myself. It was just too good. "And we charge for the certificates?" I was scarily being myself in front of him and not caring. Hopefully, David would agree to signing them!

"Yeah exactly, if you've sold your tickets already. This could be an add-on, yeah."

"Yeah! We really need to raise more money to meet the target. Thanks, Dad!"

Dad blushed and puffed his chest a little, and Mustafa looked up from his screen. Oh man, I'd just called him Dad out loud.

Dad nudged Mustafa, "Go on!"

Mustafa opened the glove compartment. "Uhhh . . . I've got the Year Seven trip to France so can't join the shoot-out." He leaned over Dad and handed me a fiver. "I can't buy a ticket, but you can take a shot for me if you want?"

I stared at him. So he had a good reason for not buying a ticket. And even though Dad had probably given him the money, he was still donating it towards the fundraiser. I was impressed. I'd have done the exact same if I couldn't go.

"Okay, thanks. I'll put this into the pot," I said when I realized he was looking at me expecting a reply. I was probably acting weird and should go. I looked up to see if Sami was still waiting. He was leaning against the railings and writing in his exercise book—probably doing his homework.

"I'll bring the certificates tomorrow. How many shall I print?" asked Dad, switching on the engine.

"Uhh . . . can I message you? I don't know how many off the top of my head."

"Yeah, no problem. Speak to you soon." He looked in his rearview mirror and signaled. That was a hint telling me to leave. I walked off, watching the car pull into the traffic on the road.

He was going off with his real family and leaving me standing there. Again. But he did seem to be trying.

Chapter 33

Later that evening, I sat on Ahmed's bed looking out the window chatting to Sami and Mark about the certificates on a WhatsApp video call.

"It doesn't look like we've made enough money," I said. "Even with *all* the penalty shoot-out tickets and loads of spectator tickets sold. We're still about one thousand and seven hundred pounds short. We're gonna have to get these certificates printed."

"Aadam said the lawyer is making a fuss about the time he needs to work on his case and he's worried he might cancel if we can't get the money by Thursday." Sami sounded flat.

Mark chipped in. "If we can sell these certificates, Sami, we'll make it."

"We've already asked David to do so much, he might not even say yes," said Sami. "But if he does, everyone will want one."

"Yeah," I said, looking out at the street of identical semidetached houses. "I messaged some of our year and they all said they wanted one. I mean, who wouldn't want a signed David Mora certificate? Will you ask him if he'll do it? Maybe post a note into his letterbox?"

"Yeah, 'course I will. We could charge ten pounds for each one," said Mark.

"Yeah, but what about all the kids who can't afford that?" I said. "I know my mum would struggle to pay for a penalty kick *plus* a certificate. Sami's too, right?"

Sami nodded.

"Hey! What if we only give signed certificates to the kids who get a goal?" I sat up. "I mean how many kids will actually score? Maybe one or two? And hopefully David won't mind signing just a few then? BUT it would mean we'll sell *more* spectator tickets if we say there's a presentation and certificate for goal scorers? People would wanna stay for more than penalty kicks? The parents would love a presentation, right?"

"Yeah, that's what we need to do." Sami smiled. "All right, well message your dad to get some printed, then."

"All right!"

After we'd all hung up, I googled sample certificates and copied all the words, changing the text to "I scored a goal against David Mora!" Then I messaged Dad the number we'd need printed and what we wanted them to say.

My phone started buzzing in my hand. It was Dad. I pressed the green button to answer.

"Listen, Ali. I need to speak to you," he said.

"Uhhh . . . okay." I peeked out my bedroom door, trying to figure out if anyone was around upstairs. I couldn't hear anything, so I jumped onto my bed.

"Ali, I haven't stopped thinking about what you said when you came to my house, and I need to give you my side of the story."

"What story?" I jumped off my bed and started pacing.

"We didn't get to talk properly when you visited me . . . Look, you were very young when I left . . ."

"Yeah, I know."

"And your mum and me were fighting all the time. I didn't want to leave you and not see you again, but I couldn't explain to you when you were five—you wouldn't have understood. At the time, I had no job or house of my own, and I already had a baby to look after and another wife who I was going to move in with, so it was best to leave you with your mum. I knew she'd do a good job."

My body tensed, and I could feel anger threading through my veins. "She did a wicked job." I glanced in the mirror as I walked past it. If I was Hulk I'd be green right now.

"She did."

Yeah, no thanks to you, I thought.

"Anyway, look," Dad continued. "I did what I thought was best for you at the time. I thought you'd be better off with some stability instead of being passed around between me and your mum. It wasn't the right decision. But I was young and a bit stupid."

You said it! I wished I could say that out loud.

I think Dad sensed I was agreeing with the stupid part because of my silence. "Okay, so, uhhh . . . I'll see you tomorrow after school with the certificates?"

I flumped on my bed and stared at my socks. "Yeah."

"Okay, beta. See you, then." And he hung up.

I swiped my hand across my forehead. A dull headache had come on. It didn't matter what Dad's reasons were. He still went missing and didn't think about us until now. Although, I had to admit he *was* trying. But could I trust him? Was he going to stick around this time or leave again as soon as he got the chance?

My phone buzzed, and I sighed. What now? I lifted it in front of my face, but it wasn't Dad; Mark had sent a message:

M: Mum's gone ballistic

I swiped into our chat while he was still typing.

A: Why? Did you show her the CCTV already???

M: No! She saw that selfie we all took at footy. She knows I'm still playing football with Aadam, the refugee thief—that's what she calls him—and now she's grounded me!

Mark carried on:

M: We have to come up with a plan to get Callum out the house. He's been ill and hasn't been out at all today. I HAVE to show her the CCTV!!!

Sami started typing in the chat.

> **S:** We'll come to yours.

I laughed and typed:

> **A:** To do what? Get beaten up?

Sami carried on typing:

> **S:** When Callum sees us on the drive, he'll come out to shout at us!

I replied:

> **A:** Or kill us 💀

Mark started typing . . .

> **M:** I won't let him come near you. When r u coming?

This could end up going really badly, but if it worked out, we'd not only expose Callum, we'd also clear Aadam's name and get our epic pool life back.

Me and Sami replied at the exact same time:

> A: Now?

> S: Now?

I grinned. Brothers were doing this. I'd have to tell Mum I'd left my homework at Mark's house or something.

Sami sent another message:

> S: Aadam's coming too. He's not taking no for an answer. Said he'll be our backup.

Sami and Aadam walked down the road on either side of me. Both of them looked as anxious as I felt. Sami was biting his bottom lip, and Aadam had his hands in his pockets and his hood on, but you could still see his crinkly brow.

What would Callum do when he saw us back here and this time *with Aadam*? My mouth was so dry, and there was no way I could ask for any water when we got there. I gulped and tried to focus on the pretty green canopy of trees and the birds chittering in the evening sun.

As we got halfway down Mark's road, I messaged him:

> A: We're almost outside. Now what?

Mark called right away. I put the call on speaker and turned the volume down a little, looking around to check no one was outside their gates listening. But nobody was around as usual. Phew.

"It's Mark," I whispered. Sami and Aadam stopped walking and leaned in.

"Ali, listen. Press the buzzer and I'll let you all in. But wait at the bottom of the steps when you get up the drive . . . Hello? Are you listening?"

"Yeah, yeah, I am. We all are."

"Okay, so, once I've seen you come up the drive, I'll leave the door wide open and shout your names and say 'What you doing here?' And then I'll run down the steps to chat to you. Hopefully Callum will follow 'cause he's a nosy git and will want to tell us off. And when he does, you and me, Ali, will run inside and lock the door so he can't get back in."

"Errr, what about Sami and Aadam? Are we just gonna leave them outside?" I said, looking at them.

Aadam leaned in closer to put his mouth to the phone. "Don't worry, we'll distract him."

"How?" asked Sami.

"Yeah, how?" I asked.

"We can run off around the garden. I know it so well, I can hide with Sami easily. They've also got lots of trees we can climb."

"I'm not climbing up a tree!" Sami said, a bit too loudly.

I looked around to check no one had come out. Still quiet. What a good street—or bad, if you were in danger. No one would even hear—or care.

"Okay, listen," said Mark. "When me and Ali are in, I'll shout at Callum before I close the door and say something about him not coming in. Then he'll try to get in, won't he? So that'll give you time to hide."

"Okay, yeah." Sami blew out. "We can do that."

"So, what we gonna do inside?" I asked Mark.

"You're gonna back me up with Mum so we can make sure she listens and doesn't walk off. She has to see the CCTV. She won't let 'the refugees' in so this is our best bet to show her the truth."

"Okay," I said, looking at Sami and Aadam. "We're

coming. Get ready." My stomach rolled as I put the phone back in my jeans.

"We don't even have anything to protect us," said Sami, with his hands in his pockets.

"We've got Allah," said Aadam. "He got us this far, didn't he?"

Sami smiled and looked down and started praying in Arabic. So I prayed Ayatul Kursi, a Quranic verse, and asked Allah to make this easy for us. And then Aadam did the same. *If anyone comes out now and hears three boys in hoods praying in Arabic, we'll definitely get arrested.*

I looked around again as we approached the massive driveway gates and pressed the buzzer.

A few seconds later, the gates clacked and started opening into the driveway. My muscles tensed, and I could feel my heart racing faster.

"Keep an eye out for him. Be ready," said Aadam.

I nodded, and Sami readjusted his hood.

We walked along the sweeping drive, keeping an eye out for Callum running out to us with an axe or something. The perfect house emerged in front of us, and I could hear my heartbeat in my ears.

We stopped in front of the steps and waited for Mark to come.

A few seconds passed, and nothing happened.

"What if Callum heard Mark talking to us and now he's locked him up?" said Sami.

"Stop it, man!" I said. My head was spinning with images of Callum doing something to Mark. What would we do? We were locked *inside* the gates as well!

"Do you know the gate code to get out?" I asked Aadam.

"They changed it after I left, I think. Right, Sami?"

"Yeah, Mark told us. Don't you remember?" Sami hunched his shoulders and scraped his trainers on the paving as if he was cleaning dog poo off them.

"WHAT ARE YOU DOING HERE?!'"

I jumped. It was Mark, trying to sound surprised. Oh, God.

I glanced at Sami and Aadam and blew out. "You ready?"

"Yeah," said Aadam. "We're gonna run that way." He pointed at the big lawn that led to the pool room.

"Okay," said Sami, getting his arms in position to run for his life.

Chapter 34

Mark emerged at the top of the stone stairs and ran down in his tracksuit. "I told him you were here. He's coming." Mark stopped at the bottom of the steps and turned to check. "Here, this is the gate fob to get out." He handed a plastic rectangle with two buttons on it to Sami. "I was just looking for it."

So that's why he took ages. Clever.

"Just press the left button and they'll open. Run off as soon as you see him and get home." Mark stepped aside near the staircase wall and pulled my arm. "Ali, come over here, so we can run up this side, away from him, when he comes down the middle."

Sure enough, Callum appeared. He was wearing a bathrobe and slippers, so he definitely wasn't armed and ready to kill us, phew! "WHAT THE HELL DO YOU THINK YOU'RE DOING HERE? GEMMA, CALL THE POLICE! THEY'RE TRESPASSING!"

"Get ready," I whispered.

As he got to the last-but-one step, Mark shouted, "Run!"

Aadam and Sami turned and split, and I raced behind Mark, up two stone steps at a time.

"GET BACK HERE!" Callum screamed.

My heart was pounding triple time as I got to the top, dashed across the porch, and through the double doors. Mark let me in and then grabbed the door handle. "You're not coming back in, Callum!" he screamed, and slammed the door shut. He turned the key in the lock and pulled it out, shoving it into his tracksuit pocket. "Clever, eh?" he said, grinning.

I stared at the door, stepping back, expecting Callum to start pounding it any second.

"Looks like he's gone after Sami and Aadam," said Mark.

They did have a head start, but what if the gates didn't open? I gulped.

"What are you—" Mark's mum was at the top of the stairs wearing a black T-shirt and leggings, holding what looked like a bottle of red nail varnish like my sister wore.

"Mum, me and Ali need to show you the CCTV."

"What?" She didn't look happy. "Get him outta here. You're in big trouble, Mark!"

"How much money went missing?" Mark asked his mum.

"The money that you think Aadam stole," I added.

Mark clambered up the stairs and grabbed her arm. "Mum, I'm begging you, just come and see."

She frowned and let Mark lead her down the stairs, all the while looking at me as if I was the dirt on her shoe.

He led her to the broom cupboard behind the central staircase. "Ali, come in," Mark said, sounding muffled. I walked to where his Mum stood with her hands on her hips and watched Mark fiddle around with the settings.

He pulled out his phone and checked something, then entered the date and time before pressing play. He stepped back so we could see the screen, which sat on the third shelf from the top.

"Come closer," he said to his mum.

"So this shows Aadam, does it?" His mum walked

into the cupboard, which was lined with bare shelves, and folded her arms. I followed.

The screen showed the boot room at the back of the house near the pool room. No one was in it.

"It's just an empty room. Stop wasting my time, Mark!"

"Shhh, Mum, just wait a few seconds. You'll see."

I folded my arms too, wondering if Sami and Aadam had made it out onto the street. Would Callum chase them the whole way in his slippers? He did look angry enough.

On the screen, the boot room door opened, and Callum entered holding a file box. He peeked through the open door and then nudged it shut behind him, holding the handle to close it quietly.

Mark's mum leaned in closer, and I stood on my toes to see the screen more clearly.

Callum put the file box on the worktop and opened it, revealing what looked like cash.

"That's my money for the building work . . . ," said Mark's mum.

Callum then picked up a rucksack with a Syria flag on it from the floor and dumped it next to the file box. Aadam's bag.

I felt my jaw drop to somewhere near the top of my chest.

Callum unzipped the rucksack, then took a wad of cash from the file box. He put one wad inside and zipped the bag up, then dropped it back onto the floor.

"That's the one thousand pounds we found in his bag," said Mark's mum, sounding wounded.

Callum then took a jacket from a coat hook and four more wads of cash from the file box and stuffed them all into different pockets.

He put the jacket over his arm, grabbed the file box, and opened the door, peeking left and right, before leaving and shutting the door behind him.

"I was wondering why he was getting his winter jacket dry-cleaned in the middle of May. We do everything together . . . It was the only way he could get away with it . . ."

Mark rubbed his mum's back. "How much cash was it, Mum?"

She turned to look at him. Her face was paler than I'd ever seen it, and tears brimmed in her eyes. "Five thousand pounds," she whispered, as if her voice was stuck in her throat. She swallowed and cleared it. "It was cash I'd taken out to pay the builder for the work he had to do on the swimming pool shower room. But we only found one thousand pounds in Aadam's bag and the other four thousand pounds was missing." She tucked her hair behind her ear. "Callum said that Aadam must've been taking chunks each time he came . . . but *he* stole it in one go and made it all up." She looked down and shuffled her feet. "I knew something was off. He kept talking about getting married next month and I kept saying it's too soon."

"Married?" said Mark, his eyes wide with shock.

Mark's mum straightened her shoulders. Her nostrils flared, and her hands trembled. "He took the money and was willing to get an innocent young boy in trouble for it! He told me I shouldn't call the police because it'd take too long if they went through the courts 'cause he's not legal and we might get in trouble for employing an illegal immigrant!" She pushed past Mark as she stormed out and up the stairs, bashing each step as she went.

I looked at Mark. "Well done, mate. You cleared Aadam's name." I patted him on the arm.

Mark closed his eyes. "I did it . . . finally. Mum knows what scum he is now." He looked at me. "Come on, we better go and see what's happening outside!"

Mark reset the screen to show the live cameras, and I watched, fascinated by all the various rooms that were covered.

"Come on," said Mark when he'd finished, and we headed out of the broom cupboard, Mark closing the door behind him.

We'd just made it to the front door when his mum shouted, "Mark!" We both turned. His mum was stomping downstairs with a black plastic bag in her hand. "Callum's clothes." She went into the kitchen and came back with some scissors, then she started cutting up the contents of the bag. Snipping every piece repeatedly.

Mark looked at me and grinned, and I couldn't help but grin too. Callum was getting wrecked!

"Throw this outside the gates for me." She twisted the top of the bag. "I'm just gonna get his phone." She chucked the balled-up black bag at Mark and headed into the kitchen.

Mark locked eyes with me, and we both ran to the front door. I took the black bag from him as he unlocked the door, and we raced down the stone steps. "Ali, call the police!"

"Eh? For real?"

"Yeah!" He panted as we ran. "Mum'll be out in a second. Tell the police he's gonna hit us or something to make sure they come straightaway. They won't come if we tell them he stole money weeks ago. We need to make it sound urgent. Oh, and tell them we're only thirteen." He put his hand out to take the black bag from me. "I want to make sure she shows the CCTV to the police while she's angry, and not to *him*. He could delete it, and this is our chance to get him arrested for stealing from her and framing Aadam!"

"Okay." I pulled my phone out of my pocket and dialed 999.

Chapter 35

"*Where is he?*" Mark's mum stormed towards the front gate, focused straight ahead.

I backed up into the hedge. "Uhhh ... I have to go ... He's gonna hit us. We're only thirteen! Please help and come soon!" I pressed the red button and finished my call to the emergency operator.

"WHERE ARE YOU, CALLUM?" Mark's mum's arms swung like two pendulums as she marched down the long driveway with his phone in her hand.

I ran after her, and soon spotted Mark hovering near the exotic-looking palm trees about three meters from the gate. He was recording Callum swearing at Aadam and Sami, who were on the road side of the gate. Aadam was holding the gate fob out, and it looked like he was pressing close every time Callum punched the code in to open it.

Callum stood with his legs planted wide, one hand fisted by his side.

"YOU LYING SCUMBAG!" Mark's mum screamed, and Callum turned. His face was the color of raw salmon.

"Gemma, get me the gate fob, these bloody illegals have somehow got one and aren't letting me get through. In fact, switch off the electrics and I'll get through manually."

Mark's mum walked right up to Callum. Her nose was almost touching his.

"Mark, pass me the bag." She stuck her arm out, and Mark ran up and put the black bag in her hand.

"What are you doing, you silly woman?" Callum said, his lips pressed together in a white slash. "We haven't got time for this!"

"Seeing right through you." Mark's mum stepped back and opened the top of the black bag. She lifted it over his head and spilled his cut-up clothes all over him.

Callum's jaw dropped, and he stepped back, looking at Mark's mum and then at Mark and me.

Sami and Aadam cheered from behind the gate.

"What have they told you? IT AIN'T TRUE!" His arms were splayed, and the color was draining out of his face.

Mark's mum pressed her gate fob, and it clacked and started opening. "I know you're a LIAR! I know you're a THIEF and I know you're SCUM!" she screamed, and lunged forward with each word while Callum stepped back in shock until he was on the private road.

Just then, a police car with blue flashing lights but no siren screeched to a halt. They came!

I let out a breath. Sami blew out too, and Aadam put his hand to his chest. Mark ran out onto the road.

"Ah, about time too," Callum said, turning to the police officers. "They were trespassing!" He pointed at Aadam and Sami.

A bearded police officer stepped out of the front passenger door and looked at Callum in his fluffy blue bathrobe.

"We've been told you've been exhibiting threatening and violent behavior towards these kids," he said, while a female police officer got out of the car and came round to join him.

"You what? Nah, it's them you want," Callum said, laughing nervously.

"Oh, I'm so glad you're here!" Mark's mum rushed up to them. "I've got CCTV evidence and everything. He stole a lot of money from me—five thousand pounds to be precise—and then accused these innocent kids. He's made a fool of me!" Tears welled in her eyes, and her voice broke.

"WHAT ARE YOU SAYING, WOMAN? I HAVEN'T BEEN STEALING FROM NO ONE!" Callum sprang at Mark's mum, his arms fisted, and she jumped back.

The two police officers got in between and pushed him aside. As the male police officer put his hand around Callum's wrist, Callum slapped it away. "GET OFF ME!"

"Sir, if you don't calm down, we're going to have to arrest you."

"Arrest me for what?!" Callum shoved the officer hard in his chest.

The female officer clasped her handcuffs and grabbed one of Callum's arms, while the bearded officer grabbed the other, then they pulled them behind his back and cuffed him.

Callum started squirming. "I haven't done anything! You can't do this!"

Mark locked eyes with me and smirked.

The bearded officer gripped Callum's arms to stop him from moving. "You are getting violent, and for your own and our safety, I am arresting you for assaulting a police officer."

"I was just defending myself!" Callum wriggled. "I ain't done nothing wrong!"

The female officer opened the back passenger door and said, "You do not have to say anything. But it may harm your defense if you do not mention when questioned something which you later rely on in court. Anything you do say may be given in evidence." She shoved Callum's head into the car and then nudged his back. It was like a scene from *Traffic Cops*.

Mark ran up to his mum and put his arm around her. She put her head on his shoulder.

I closed my eyes and breathed out, grateful that Callum had got himself arrested without any of us getting hurt.

And I'd actually helped.

And got something right.

Chapter 36

Friday, 4 p.m.—we were ready. It was finally the charity penalty shoot-out day and the whole school was buzzing with excitement. The last two days had whooshed by, with meetings with the student council and teachers to get everything sorted in time. Mark had taken Wednesday and Thursday off to be with his mum after what had happened with Callum. Even while he was dealing with all that, he'd managed to ask David if he'd sign a few certificates. It was good to see Mark back in school, his blue eyes sparkling and that cheeky grin back on his face again.

The PTA was here and had set up stalls selling drinks and snacks that parents had donated. The PE teachers were letting in the spectators and separating them from the kids who were going to take the penalties. People were sitting on the grass with their juice cartons, fizzy-drink cans, and crisps packets at least five lines deep all around the football pitch; some had brought foldable chairs and made themselves comfortable. The drama department had even put up a little stage for speeches. I looked around, wondering who was going to speak.

Aadam was on the sidelines, beaming, even though we hadn't made the full target. We'd all felt really bad about it. We needed a miracle to make up the money now.

David hadn't arrived yet, but we still had half an hour to go before kickoff.

Mark pulled his phone out of his pocket. "It's Mum," he said, looking at the screen and then swiping. I looked at Sami, but he was busy waving at his little sister in the crowd.

"Yeah," said Mark. "Just come in through the normal car park and you'll see loads of people. Head this way and I'm standing near the goal . . . okay." He put the phone back in his shorts pocket and looked at me and Sami. "She was at the police station giving her statement."

"Seriously?" said Sami, his eyebrows high.

"Yeah. Callum was locked up for two nights 'cause of the way he kicked off when the police came and then again in the car, so they're definitely charging him for assaulting a police officer. And now she's given her statement and dropped off the CCTV recording, he's gonna be charged for theft as well." He smiled and looked at me. "Thanks for calling the police, by the way. Mum's finally seen what Callum's really like, and after seeing him push that police officer, she was determined to tell them everything about what a nasty, racist bully he is as well!"

"Mate, it was all your brainpower." I shrugged.

"Yeah, Aadam said he wants to get you something to thank you for clearing his name," said Sami.

"I don't need nothing!" said Mark, his cheeks going pink.

"Yeah, *I* should be giving Aadam something." We all turned to see Mark's mum in a floaty pink dress and strappy heels that were digging into the grass as she walked. "Where is he?" she asked.

"Uhhh . . . over there," said Sami, pointing to Aadam.

"I just have to say sorry . . . to you all." She took off her big black sunglasses. "I was tricked into believing some really bad things about you kids, even though I *knew* you were good and loyal friends of my Mark." She looked down at her shoes. "I was so stupid to have listened to him." She looked up at us. "Anyway, I just wanted to say I was wrong for how I treated you." She put her sunglasses back on and unclipped her big leather handbag. "I want to donate two thousand pounds to the fund for Aadam."

"No way!" I grinned.

Sami's mouth fell. "This means we'll have raised enough money to pay for his fees *and* have extra left over! Thank you!"

"Yesss!" Mark pumped his fist. "Thanks, Mum!"

"It's the least I can do. Maybe he can buy something nice for himself if there's any spare." Mark's mum smiled.

I looked into the crowd for Aadam and waved him over. He was now sitting with Ahmed, my mum and sister, and Sami's parents. Someone waved from two rows behind.

It was Dad.

He was here too . . .

But Mustafa . . . was away on that school trip to France. And Dad wasn't with Ahmed either.

Was it possible he'd come . . . for me?

Just for me? My spine tingled. Whoa. He *was* here just for ME! Maybe he really did want to be my dad too.

"Hey, guys!" We all turned to see David in his yellow goalie kit. "Ready to score some goals?"

"YEAH!" Mark, Sami, and I said together.

Mrs. Webster ran over. "Hi, David! Would you like a drink?"

"Maybe later, thanks." He waved his bottle of water. "I've got this for now."

"Ah, no worries. We've also prepared some cold towels if you get too hot!" She pointed at a cooler box near the stage.

"Oh, perfect, thanks!" He smiled.

Mrs. Webster stared at him as if she wanted to ask something. "I'll just go back to seating the spectators." She stopped and looked at him, holding out her phone, opened her mouth and closed it, then jogged off. Was she going to ask him for a selfie and now was trying to play it cool? It was so funny seeing the teachers losing their minds over David.

David nudged me with his shoulder. "You wanna take the first kick?"

My whole face erupted into the cheesiest grin. "Yeah, man!" I looked around. "Where's the ball?"

Mrs. Hack came over wearing the school tracksuit and a cap. I did a double take. She looked a lot younger in a cap and so like Grace. "Hi, David, welcome to Heath Academy. Would you like a drink?"

"No, I'm good, thanks." He waved his water bottle again.

"I'm just going to introduce you." She pointed at the stage. "I was wondering if you would like to say anything later?"

"Actually, I might just talk the kids through penalties before we start, if that's okay?"

"Oh, that would be amazing!" Mrs. Hack smiled. "Would you like to do it from the stage? That way everyone can hear you?"

David went a little red. "Uhh . . . I could, sure."

"David is here!" Mr. Clarke shouted, running over, out of breath. His grin was huge as he stepped forward to shake David's hand.

"Good afternoon, everyone!" Mrs. Hack had climbed up onto the stage and was standing in front of a microphone.

The bustle from the crowds quieted, and we turned

to watch her. "Welcome to Heath Academy for this incredibly momentous occasion. We have gathered here today because of three Year Eight Heath Academy students who we are all incredibly proud of." She looked down at me, Sami, and Mark and smiled. Aadam, Mum, Ahmed, Mark's mum, and Sami's parents all cheered and clapped loud, leading everyone else to start clapping too.

I looked down at my football boots, embarrassed.

Mrs. Hack continued. "We have come together exactly one month before Refugee Week to help a member of our community here in Stockport. These three Year Eights came to us and asked if we would help Aadam al-Rashid, who is like family to one of them. And we of course wanted to, because Aadam deserves the same opportunities as any Heath Academy student does. Aadam is sixteen and he came from Syria because his country has been destroyed by war and is now unsafe for him to return to. But, when he got here, instead of being welcomed, Aadam was wrongly accused of being an adult and told he had to return to Syria. And so, we are here today to help ensure that doesn't happen and to let Aadam know that we support him and that he is very welcome. AND I am delighted to tell you we have the AMAZING Mr. David Mora here, who is helping us too! What a *wonderful* way to go into the half-term holidays!"

Some trumpet fanfare music played out from the speakers, and everyone cheered and burst into applause.

"David is now going to give our students a few tips before we begin the penalty shoot-out. Over to you, David!" Mrs. Hack clapped as she walked off the stage.

David stepped up onto the stage and cleared his throat. Everyone fell silent.

"I met these young boys by chance, and like the true heroes they are, they were stopping someone from damaging my car." He looked down at us and smiled.

I felt my cheeks warm.

"And so when they asked me to help Sami's older brother, I jumped at the chance. I'm very happy to be here with you all."

Everyone cheered louder than before.

"I'll now just give you a few tips before we begin." He turned to the kids sitting in front of the stage in their school sports kits. "For me, penalty kicks are all about reflexes," said David. "I've trained myself to watch closely and predict how you might move. But for *you* it's about power, and power comes from sticking to your decision. Are you going to try to curve the ball or shoot straight? How are you going to confuse me?"

The whole field was silent and still, everyone mesmerized to be in the company of *the* actual David Mora.

He continued. "The legend Alan Shearer said he used to decide which side of the net he'd aim for *before* he did his run-up. So decide where you're gonna kick, and then go for it! Right, let's start!" David rubbed his hands and stepped off the stage, patting me on my back as he walked off. Everyone stood and cheered him.

"DAVID MORA JUST TOUCHED MY SHIRT!" I shouted to Sami and Mark over the noise.

We all grinned and followed him.

"Can you get all the kids in a line, please? We've got a lot of penalties to get through!" David said to Mrs. Hack.

Mr. Clarke jogged over with a netted bag full of footballs. "Hi, David. Shall we set up?"

"Yeah, I'm ready." David smiled. He looked over at me and Sami and Mark and then jogged off into goal.

The crowd cheered as he waved at them. It was as if we'd brought a football stadium to school. Amazing.

Mr. Clarke handed me a ball, and I put it in

position and took a deep breath. Something clicked in my brain, and I turned. "Actually, get Aadam," I said to Sami. "He should have the first kick."

"Good idea!" Sami waved Aadam over.

Aadam stood a few meters from the ball and stared at David. He shook out his hands and legs, then ran at the ball and kicked it hard towards the top left corner. David almost got a finger to the ball but not quite, and it hit the back of the net.

"GOALLLL!" we all cheered, and the whole school roared.

What a start! Aadam was just too good.

I waved at Sami to go next. He fist-bumped me and put his ball in place. He closed his eyes and took a deep breath.

"Get on with it!" someone shouted. I looked behind us. It was Nathan. The idiot.

Sami looked over and rubbed his neck. It seemed Nathan had got to him *again*. He ran to the ball, then booted it high over the goal.

"OHHHHHH!" everyone groaned.

Sami grinned at me and shrugged. I whooped, proud he didn't care what Nathan thought.

Mr. Clarke handed me another ball. I was next.

I put the ball down and stepped back. My heart was beating triple time—so hard and so fast I could feel it throb in my ears.

David winked at me, and I smiled. I looked right and left and then straight ahead before kicking it, hoping I'd confused him and he'd dive out of goal. Instead, David lunged forward and caught it.

"AHHHHH!" everyone said.

But it was epic. I felt as if I was playing for Man U. I ran up to the goal and fist-bumped David. "I missed a penalty. I'm a proper England footballer now!"

David laughed as I ran to the sidelines and joined Sami and Aadam.

Mark stepped forward and took a deep breath. This was goalkeeper versus goalkeeper. I wondered if Mark would outsmart David.

Mark jogged backwards, and I heard a wolf whistle. That had to be Grace. I looked around but couldn't see her through all the spectators.

Mark put his thumb up at the crowd and then ran straight to the ball, kicked the ball hard left, and missed. "And that's why I'm better in goal!" he shouted as he ran off grinning. The crowd laughed.

A Year Seven kid stepped up next, wearing his full

England kit. The line behind him snaked all the way to the end of the pitch and back around. What a moment.

We did this.

≡

After a Year Ten kid had taken the final penalty and the certificates had been presented to the few who'd managed to score, the whole crowd started cheering, "DAVID, DAVID, DAVID!"

David stepped forward and took a bow, and me, Sami, and Mark went to thank him.

Mrs. Hack came over. "David, could we please present you with a gift?"

"Oh, there's no need!" David blushed.

"Come on, it'll be quick!" Mrs. Hack gestured him to follow her onto the stage. "We'd just like to thank David," she said into the mic, "for taking the time to support Aadam and our school community, for coaching our penalty scorers, and for just being brilliant!" She took a turquoise box with a white ribbon on it from Mrs. Webster and handed it to David.

Everyone burst into the loudest applause I'd ever heard. I wanted to cover my ears.

"Hey, Ali!" It was Dad, coming towards me from the crowd.

I stepped back. *Not now, please. Don't ruin this moment for me.*

"I just wanted to tell you that I'm so proud of you. Your mum has raised an amazing young man. You have the heart of a lion." He put his hand to his chest, and his eyes welled up. "I see how bright you shine, and I can't tell you how much it pleases me. Look how you help others. I hope Mustafa turns out to be like you."

I gulped and tried to stop my own eyes from brimming. He'd said he was proud of me. He'd said he hoped Mustafa would turn out like *me*! Oh my Wotsits.

"Thanks, Dad." My voice barely came out.

He rubbed my shoulder. "I'll see you later?"

"Yeah," I said. "Yeah, you will."

Dad put his hands in his jeans pockets and strolled off. Had that really just happened?

"Hi!" A guy in a white shirt and smart trousers walked over. "I'm from *Manchester Evening News*," he said. "Could I get a photo of you all together for the newspaper?"

David smiled. "Yeah, sure!"

We all gathered in the goal and put our fists together.

"Smile!" said the man from the newspaper.

"Cheesy biscuits," I said, and we all laughed at the camera.

Epilogue

"*Pencil dive!*" Mark ran up to the pool edge, clipped his arms tight to his sides, and jumped in, keeping his feet together.

"Star-jump dive!" I stretched my arms and legs wide and jumped in feetfirst, splatting hard through the surface of the water before swimming to the side. I turned to see Sami turning his back to the pool.

"Backwards dive!" He squatted and fell backwards, tucking his legs in before flipping in the air and diving into the water.

"Nice!" I shouted.

Aadam ran to the pool with his arms tucked behind his back. "Belly flop dive!" He jumped and landed horizontally on his front, creating a massive splash.

We all laughed as he surfaced.

"All right, I reckon Sami won that round," said Mark, wiping water from his eyes.

"Yeah, definitely," said Aadam, holding on to the side of the pool.

I fist-bumped Sami. "Yeah, you champion!"

The double doors to the pool room opened. Mark's mum came down the steps with four pizza boxes.

"Oh, thanks, Mum!" said Mark, climbing out from the poolside. I followed.

"Thanks, Aunty," I said.

She smiled at us. "So, when's David taking you all on a tour of the grounds?" she asked.

"Next Saturday," said Sami, beaming so wide I almost saw his gums.

"Do you want to have a little party over here afterwards?" she asked, taking the boxes to the table in front of the open patio doors. There was a newspaper on top of them. "Or do you want to eat out at the Trafford Centre?" She turned to me. "I was just chatting to your mum, Ali, and we're planning on getting together with Sami's mum to get some stuff together to send to Aadam's mum in Syria." She smiled at Aadam. "Maybe I could talk to her when you next call and tell her what a brilliant, well-mannered, hardworking son she has?"

"She would like that." Aadam smiled.

"Oh." She grabbed the newspaper from on top of the pizza boxes. "Look at this article all about the shoot-out and your journey, Aadam." She flicked through the pages, and we all gathered around her to see the piece the man in the smart trousers from *Manchester Evening News* had written.

"Oh, wow!" Sami elbowed Aadam. "Look at your face in the paper! And you almost didn't let him interview you!"

"I was shy!" Aadam's face reddened.

"You'll have to frame that," I said, nudging him.

"You didn't have to tell the journalist I gave you the final amount, you know." Mark's mum tapped Aadam's arm and blushed. "It was so generous of you to donate the leftover five hundred pounds to the unaccompanied minor refugee center."

Aadam shrugged. "I had enough to pay my lawyer, and so the extra money has gone towards buying the kids there a laptop for their studies."

"Oh, that's lovely," said Mark's mum. "Well done."

"No, it's thanks to you," Aadam said, pushing his wet hair off his face.

"What if the journalist comes to the tour of the grounds as well?" Sami asked.

"Then there will be more photos of all of us in the paper!" Aadam turned the page over to see what was behind it, and then back to the feature on him and the shoot-out.

"Let's all eat out after the tour," said Mark, his eyes sparkling with excitement. "This already feels like a party!"

"Uhhh . . . I can't," I said, and scratched my head. Everyone turned to look at me. "I'm going out with my dad."

"Your dad?" said Sami.

"Yeah, he's taking me to see his old footy club."

"Oh wow, so—from a professional ground to where people start their playing career," said Aadam, his hands on his hips, looking impressed.

"The whole journey in one afternoon," said Mark's mum, laying out the pizza boxes on the table for each of us.

"Yeah," I said, smiling. Mark's mum had let us back in, and I realized that maybe I should let Dad back in too. Maybe bad relationships could get repaired.

Although the last few weeks had been horrible because of Callum, and meeting Mustafa for the first time, and seeing Dad after so long, they'd also been kind of cool. If Callum hadn't stolen the money, we'd never have felt bad enough to organize a fundraiser for Aadam. We'd never have had a reason to speak to David and get him to help us. Mark wouldn't have been able to get rid of nasty Callum for good. Dad would never have had a reason to help with the certificates or spend time with me, as I wouldn't have let him. He might never have told me I was good enough and that he was proud of me. And we'd never be getting a private tour of a Premiership football club!

Getting kicked out of Mark's house was probably the best thing to have happened to us! We were properly living our best lives now.

Glossary

Akhi: My brother.

Asar: The afternoon prayer (one of the five compulsory Islamic daily prayers).

As-salaamu Alaikum: Peace be upon you (a Muslim greeting).

Auntyji: A respectful term for an aunt or an older woman.

Ayatul Kursi: The 255th verse in the second chapter of the Quran. Muslims believe it is the greatest protection and recite it to protect themselves from harm and evil.

Baklawa: Thin sweet pastry made of filo dough, layered with chopped nuts, and drizzled with sugar syrup or honey.

Barfi: A fudge-like sweet made with milk and sugar and usually flavored with cardamom or nuts.

Beta: "Son" in Urdu.

Booza: A stretchy, chewy ice cream that originated in Syria, made with mastic—a natural resin that comes from the mastic tree.

Dada: Granddad on father's side (Dad's father).

Dua: A prayer or supplication asking God for help or for whatever you need.

Eid: A Muslim festival celebrated twice a year.

Inshallah: God willing (Muslims say this in place of "hopefully").

Jum'ah: Friday. The noon prayer Zuhr and the religious service before it is also called jum'ah.

Kameez: A long tunic worn over loose pleated trousers that taper around the ankles, usually worn by women of South Asian heritage.

Laddu: An Indian sweet shaped into a ball. It is made out of sugar, flour, and fat.

Leave to remain: People from outside the UK have to get this permission to stay in the UK for a certain period of time. This can be for 2–3 years, 5 years, or 10 years.

Maamoul: A soft Syrian cake stuffed with dates or nuts and dusted with icing sugar or shredded coconut.

Nani: Grandma on mother's side (Mum's mother).

Paratha: A flaky, buttery flatbread.

Qadr of Allah: The divine will and decree of Allah. Muslims believe that Allah knows everything and has decided our fate and what will happen before its time.

Salaam: Used as a greeting. It means "peace."

Tabbouleh: A fresh herb and bulgur wheat salad, with parsley being the main ingredient.

Topi: The traditional hat/skullcap Muslim men wear.

Walaikum As-salaam: "Peace be upon you too" (in response to the Muslim greeting "As-salaamu Alaikum").

Ya rabb: "Oh Lord."

Author's Note

In my previous books, the characters have had to face enormous challenges, but one thing they've always had is a family with both parents and a present and engaged father. I always wanted to write the kind of father that I wish I'd had growing up. The kind who showed up when necessary and cared enough to make difficult decisions and my characters knew would be there no matter what.

But, in this story, I wanted to explore what it feels like to grow up without a father and then have him come back into your life. How does someone navigate that situation and the emotions that arise from it? I can say from experience it isn't easy, and I wanted readers to know that families come in all sorts of shapes and whatever happens within them isn't your fault—your family members don't reflect your worth, and things will be okay regardless of how imperfect they may be.

I also wanted to shine a light on the plight of unaccompanied minors and asylum seekers. It has been eight years since I first started writing *Boy, Everywhere* in 2015, when the rhetoric around refugees was divisive and dangerous. It saddens me that it has not improved, and instead, politicians and the media are still using refugees and asylum seekers to further their own agendas.

As I write this note, the UK government is doing everything in its power to demonize refugees and is making it harder than ever for them to seek safety here. The hateful narrative stretches across Europe and the US too, with many countries taking in fewer refugees than ever before. The two questions often asked about lone young men seeking asylum have always been: Why didn't they stay in their country with their families? And why have they come alone?

Aadam's reasons for fleeing war in this story are based on real events. The majority of lone young men, like Aadam in *Kicked Out*, fled Syria because they didn't want to fight in the war. They didn't want to attack their neighbors and countryfolk, and so they left in the hope they'd escape the war and one day return to their homes and families without having harmed anyone.

Many parents send their precious young boys out of their country in the hope they'll have a better, safer future, just like Aadam's mum does. But, when asylum seekers arrive here, typically they are not welcomed and instead they are accused of lying. Asylum claims are often rejected if accounts in an interview or on paper have tiny variances in recollection. Many young boys who have lost documentation and proof of identity on their long journeys are not believed when stating their age and are told they look like adults based on visual checks, some because, like Aadam, they have wrinkled, weathered hands or faces due to the harsh, cold outdoors they've had to survive in for months. Years pass, and these children grow up without care or proper education, navigating through an adult asylum system without the support and safeguards they should have. Lawyers can sometimes exploit vulnerable people, asking for fees and suggesting legal aid is unavailable. It is inhumane to allow any of this to happen because of a slow and inefficient asylum system.

My hope is that, having read this book, readers might feel inspired to speak up against unjust laws and find out how *you* can welcome and support asylum seekers who simply arrive at our shores with the hope of living with some dignity and in safety (there's more about that on page 307, What Can We Do?). Refugee Week is a UK-wide festival that was founded in 1998 to encourage greater understanding of why people seek safety and to celebrate the contributions of refugees in the UK. It is held every year in June around World Refugee Day, which is celebrated globally. I hope this story will empower you and show you that you *can* make a difference. There are so many ways you can step up. And, schools, I hope you will also be inspired by Heath Academy and do more for Refugee Week or

World Refugee Day, or as part of your curriculum, and perhaps reach out to refugees in your own community who will no doubt appreciate the effort.

Growing up isn't easy. It can be hard to understand the world you're in and your own place in it. It's a time in your life that can really shape the choices you make. Unfortunately, there are lots of young people experiencing discrimination and microaggressions, who live with violent, controlling family members like Mark, get name-called, etc. A book can literally be life-changing when you can see yourself in it or if you realize you have something in common with those who seem or are depicted as being different from you.

The arrival of Ali's father and half brother rocks Ali's world, and he ends up questioning his self-worth. I wanted to show, through Ali, how resilient young people can be, and that how people treat you or whether they choose to be absent from your life is not a reflection of *you*. That is a reflection of their thinking and decision-making, and it has no bearing on who you are and who you will become. It takes Ali a while to realize this, and you'll have seen he really struggles on his journey to this point. But he finds the strength to continue despite the challenges he faces, and he gets there. I hope for those of you who have struggled because of the way people have treated you or left you out of their lives, you will also go on to achieve whatever you want to, even if you don't have the validation your heart desires. *You* have the power to make things happen, and no one can stop you from being your best self. Your worth does not depend on who is there for you, who loves you, and who gives you time.

I hope anyone reading *Kicked Out* will feel inspired by Ali's story and see that you have to first believe in yourself and the rest will all fall into place.

With love and hope always,

A. M. Dassu

What Can We Do?

The refugee crisis around the world is not going anywhere, and with climate change destroying entire neighborhoods, it is only going to get worse. Now is the time to start a conversation about what we need to do to build a kinder and more supportive society for those who are forced to seek refuge elsewhere. If there's one thing we should remember, it's that it could happen to any one of us.

There were 89.3 million people who were forced to flee their homes by the end of 2021. Of these, 53.2 million people had to move within their own country, and 27.1 million moved to another country in search of safety. We are constantly told refugees are a threat and that they come here illegally, when, in reality, there are no safe and lawful routes into safe countries for them to use.

The UK and Europe are not affected by the refugee crisis in the same way other countries are, despite what we're told by the media and some politicians. Countries like Turkey, Uganda, and Pakistan take in more refugees than the whole of Europe put together. Approximately 72% of refugees live in countries that are neighbors with their country of origin, and most of these are developing countries. Almost half of displaced people around the world are children, and they deserve the same access to food, water, housing, and education that we would want for ourselves, were we to find ourselves in that position. I wrote my novel *Boy, Everywhere* in response to the divisive and hateful portrayal of refugees in the news. It is a story that shows *we* are all one cruel twist of fate away from becoming refugees ourselves.

One thing we should all be reminded of and challenge when we hear it said is that you cannot be an "illegal" asylum seeker. Under international law, you have the right to apply for asylum (shelter and protection) in any of the 149 countries that have signed the 1951 Refugee Convention, including the UK. While the United States didn't sign it right away, they later signed the 1967 Protocol Relating to the Status of Refugees. These agreements between 149 countries recognize the rights of refugees and that people fleeing their homes might have to use various ways to escape and get to safety.

There are many ways we can support refugees and unaccompanied minors. Here are some ideas:

Speak up. It is hard, but we need to correct people if they say something that isn't accurate. Find out the *facts* so that if people don't agree with you because of something they've read, or seen on the news or on social media, you can challenge them on it with confidence. You can also speak out in many other ways: write to your local paper, organize an assembly at school, post on social media so everyone knows you support refugees!

Challenge racism and hateful language. Look at the language you and the people in your life use. Are you describing people in a way that might be offensive? Could some of the words you use be untrue and not applicable to a whole group of people?

Email or call your member of Congress, both your Senator and Congressional Representative. Write to tell them why you think refugees and asylum seekers deserve our protection, and ask them to make suggestions to change the law to help refugees seek safety here more easily. If you don't have your own email address, you could ask a trusted adult to email them on your behalf. Find out who represents you at congress.gov/members/find-your-member.

Reach out and support. We are so much stronger when we support each other. You can reach out in so many ways: a smile; a kind word; by volunteering; by learning some words in other languages; by learning about different cultures and the countries refugees have come from. You could also fundraise or donate money to charities; or even just raise awareness by supporting local and regional organizations or groups that provide young refugees who are unaccompanied with a safe place to heal and the support to make their futures better. In the US there are several organizations that support young refugees. For example, the Unaccompanied Refugee Minors Program works with the Catholic organization USCCB and the Lutheran organization LIRS to provide support and foster placements for young refugees. You can find out more about what they do at acf.hhs.gov/orr/programs/refugees/urm. There are seven other refugee resettlement agencies in the US that work to support refugee families as well. If you're old enough to have social media, you can share their articles/blogs/retweet their work. Your school can also become a "School of Sanctuary"—ask a teacher for help with finding out how.

Believe things will change. Discuss issues about refugees with like-minded people, but also with people who don't agree with you so they might become aware why their opinions and behavior affect others. Most of all, never lose hope. If we believe things will get better for refugees, we're more likely to want to help to make it happen.

Acknowledgments

This is the very first full-length novel that I have written *after* becoming a published author. The first two had several drafts underway before they were even bought, and so the process has been very squeezed and different. I didn't think I'd manage to get it written from concept to print-ready in just six months, while launching my World Book Day novella and with so many other commitments. And it's only thanks to the following people that I managed it.

I'd like to thank first and foremost, as always, my dear friend and confidante Catherine Coe for always reading my worst zero drafts, for being there for me, and being so very patient about all the other things I am supposed to send to you because I had to first write this. Thank you for supporting me always. I am ever thankful for you.

A huge thanks to my UK publisher, Ruth Huddleston at Old Barn Books, for buying this book before it was even written and for believing in it based on a one-page synopsis. Thanks also for making this into a series following a World Book Day title, something we both had never envisaged all those years ago when we first met. Thank you for making so many of my dreams come true and for helping to change hateful narratives through our books.

And to my UK editor, Emma Roberts, for working on *Kicked Out* with me from the chapter plan to finish. Thank you for laughing at my jokes, encouraging me in my sports-writing techniques, and for allowing me to have the space I needed to write it by juggling your very own busy schedule. I couldn't have written this book in this time frame without you. Thank you so much for believing I could do it.

A heartfelt thanks to my US publisher, Stacy Whitman at Lee and Low, for buying the book on concept and for editing it with me before contracts were even drawn up. I know you'd never normally do that, and I can't tell you how much I appreciate the way you tell me how it is and make our editing process work. Especially when you were in the middle of setting up your very own bookstore! You amaze me, and I hope I can visit you and buy lots of books from your store one day!

The desire of all three of you to work with me and your belief in my stories means so much—I am so grateful you want to share my stories with the world and do it with so much heart. THANK YOU!

To my dearest agent, Julia Churchill. You are quite literally the best thing to have happened to me this last year. Thank you for championing me, for thinking so highly of me, and for supporting me in ways that I didn't think were possible. You honestly rock, and I am so excited to work with you on the next thing.

A huge thanks to Liz Scott, my publicist at Old Barn Books, and my US publicists/marketers, Jennifer Khawam, Jenny Choy, and Shaughnessy Miller at Lee and Low, for working with me on the campaign and always finding innovative ways to get my books into the world.

A beautiful thanks to my ever-amazing illustrator Daby Ihsan and designer Sheila Smallwood, for once again choosing to work with me, and so closely, and for creating the best covers despite your already busy workloads. I can't believe we have done four covers in just three years!

A mahoosive thank-you to my dearest and most trusted feedbackers, who took time out of their busy schedules to once again read an early draft of one of my books: Sajeda Amir, I loved your live feedback; it made me smile *so* much! Caroline Fielding, thank you for reading an early draft; I always feel more at ease once I know you approve! Kathryn Evans, my dear heart, thank you for reading it when time was squeezed and for always being there. Alexandros Plasitis, thank you so much for your feedback—I loved listening to your reactions. Thank you also for connecting me with Baca and ex-colleagues who'd worked with unaccompanied minors. Thank you, Jimmy Zachariah at

Baca and Grace Ellen-Burch, for talking me through legal aid and the experience of unaccompanied minors, and for your expert eyes on the manuscript. I'm so grateful for the important work you do, and I look forward to supporting it!

Dr. Philippa East, thank you for reading when you had your own deadline and for putting me at ease. I really appreciate you. Dr. Graham Fairweather, I can't express how much your support means to me. David Mora now almost catches Aadam's penalty because of you, and the newspaper feature is all thanks to you! Thank you to Emma Perry and Kevin Cobane for your wholehearted support and for giving me the confidence to go forward. Hannah Gold for your really helpful feedback and for encouraging me to keep going when I was doubting myself; you inspired me to show Callum's nicer side and Aadam's interests! I love our chats! And to my dearest, Louie Stowell, for fitting in a read online when you prefer to read on paper and when you had *so* much on your plate—thank you for always checking in and being there for me. Buffy's cameo in the park scene is my homage to you.

A huge thank-you to my dearest friends, Patrice Lawrence, Mo O'Hara, Liz Kessler, Sita Brahmachari, Hamida Seedat, Saima Ahsan, and everyone in the Swaggers and Venters and SCBWI-BI for being there for me through my wobbles, checking in on me, and celebrating all my good news. You really make a huge difference to my life, and I hope you know how much you all mean to me.

A massive thanks also to all my readers, parents, teachers, booksellers at Waterstones, Wonderland, Rabbit Hole, Kenilworth Books, Moon Lane, Next Page Books, Mirror Write, Chicken and Frog, A New Chapter, Kibworth Books, Write Blend, Roundtable Books, the Children's Bookshop, Pickled Pepper Books, and so many others I can't fit in here! A huge thanks to award judges, *The Week Junior*, *Kirkus Reviews*, *Booklist*, *Publishers Weekly*, *Good Housekeeping*, *The Guardian*, *Books for Keeps*, *The Bookseller*, *Bookbrunch*, and everyone who has supported me this last year. A special thanks to Kevin Cobane, Lucas Maxwell, Jenny Hawke, Rumena Akhtar, Joanna de Guia, Tamsin Rosewell, Ashley Booth, Jen O' Brien, Helen Tamblyn-Saville, Rani Tiwani, Jacqui Sydney, Karen Wallee, John Lamb, Saira Ibrahim, Ms. Z Younis, Nazia 9teaNinePercent, Scott Evans, Tom Griffiths, Hazel Pinner, Miss Defries, Kim Howard, and so many other teachers and librarians. It's been such an incredibly busy year, and I haven't had the space to breathe let alone say what I feel, so I just want to thank all of you for reading my books, shouting about them on social media, and sharing them. I see you and appreciate you dearly.

And now my family: Imran, you are the kind of father I

always wished my children would have. Thank you for supporting me and them always in everything we do. My kids—what can I say? You never cease to surprise me. Even now, on my twelfth book and probably fifteenth manuscript, you want to read my work. I honestly am *so* touched and honored by your support and love. Thank you for spending a part of your Easter holiday reading and giving me live feedback. It really was so very helpful and, yes, I owe you a new game/blog site/cupboards full of chocolate and sweets! Mustafa, thank you for telling me no one dabs anymore. Ahmed, you're quite the editor—thank you for pushing me to clarify my sentences—and, Hana, thank you for writing up all your helpful feedback, your lovely notes, hugs, and supplying me with endless biscuits and sweets! The hair train and hairbrush scenes are down to you! I only started writing because of all your love and encouragement for my stories. I love you, my babies, so much.

Thank you to Ma and Dad Dassu and the Dassus Up North for all your support, for sending food and gifts to sustain us, for understanding when I couldn't visit you because I had to work to deadlines, and appreciating how much energy this work takes. My nieces and nephews, I am so buoyed by the respect and support you give refugees in your community.

And finally, my mum. Thank you for being both my mum and dad. For giving me the confidence to believe I could do anything I put my heart to. *You* made me feel like the sky was my limit and anything was possible. Thank you for your patience and for giving me space to write when I need it. Thank you for sending food and chicken soup when I was ill. If it weren't for you, I wouldn't be where I am today.

And of course, God, thank you for absolutely *everything*: thank you for blessing me with a supportive family; brilliant friends; a writing community; wonderful publishers, librarians, booksellers, and amazing teachers; multiple awards; a World Book Day book; a computer; time; energy; and dedication to do something I not only enjoy but also makes a difference.

I didn't think I'd make it through this year because of the lack of sleep, not recovering wholly from Covid, or hit any of my several deadlines, but you helped me to somehow write and edit eight books, do two book tours across the country, multiple events, write this whole novel from concept to print in six months, while juggling a gazillion things. I look back and have no idea how. I owe you everything, always.

This is a tribute to all of you. ❤

About the Author

A. M. DASSU is the internationally acclaimed author of *Boy, Everywhere* and *Fight Back*, which have collectively been listed for more than fifty awards, including the Waterstones Children's Book Prize, the Carnegie Medal, the Little Rebels Award for Radical Fiction, the Week Junior Book Award, the American Library Association Notable Book List, and the Jane Addams Peace Book Award.

She is a director at Inclusive Minds, which is an organization for people who are passionate about inclusion, diversity, equality, and accessibility in children's literature; a patron of *The Other Side of Hope*, a literary magazine edited by immigrants and refugees, which serves to celebrate the refugee and immigrant communities worldwide; and one of the National Literacy Trust's Connecting Stories campaign authors, aiming to help inspire a love of reading and writing in children and young people.

A. M. Dassu grew up in England, dreaming of becoming a writer, but studied economics instead and worked in marketing and project management before realizing her dream. She writes books that challenge stereotypes, humanize the "other," and are full of empathy, hope, and heart. Her most recent book, *Boot It!*, was a bestselling World Book Day novel.

She has donated a part of her advances for *Kicked Out* to Baca, a UK charity that supports young people who arrive in the UK alone seeking asylum (bacacharity.org.uk/about), and to Syrians in Idlib, who lost everything once again due to the devastating earthquake in 2023.

X @a_reflective

Instagram @a.m.dassu

amdassu.com